Henry Arthur Jones

The Physician

An Original Play in Four Acts

Henry Arthur Jones

The Physician
An Original Play in Four Acts

ISBN/EAN: 9783337401290

Printed in Europe, USA, Canada, Australia, Japan

Cover: Foto ©Andreas Hilbeck / pixelio.de

More available books at **www.hansebooks.com**

HE PHYSICIAN

AN ORIGINAL PLAY IN FOUR ACTS

BY

HENRY ARTHUR JONES

AUTHOR OF

'MICHAEL AND HIS LOST ANGEL,' 'THE CRUSADERS,' 'THE CASE
OF REBELLIOUS SUSAN,' 'JUDAH,' 'THE MIDDLEMAN,' 'THE
TRIUMPH OF THE PHILISTINES,' 'THE DANCING GIRL,'
'THE TEMPTER,' 'THE ROGUE'S COMEDY,' 'THE
MASQUERADERS,' 'THE LIARS,' 'THE GOAL,'
'THE MANŒUVRES OF JANE,' ETC.

London

MACMILLAN AND CO., Limited

NEW YORK : THE MACMILLAN COMPANY

1899

Produced by Mr. Charles Wyndham at the Criterion
Theatre, London, on 25th March 1897.

PERSONS REPRESENTED

DR. LEWIN CAREY.
WALTER AMPHIEL.
REVEREND PEREGRINE HINDE.
DR. BROOKER.
STEPHEN GURDON.
JAMES HEBBINGS.
JOHN DIBLEY.
VICCARS.

EDANA HINDE.
LADY VALERIE CAMVILLE.
MRS. BOWDEN.
MRS. DIBLEY.
LOUISA PACK.
MARAH GURDON, a child.
SAUNDERS, Lady Valerie's maid.
LIZZIE, the Vicarage servant.

ACT I

SCENE—CONSULTING-ROOM AT DR. LEWIN CAREY'S,
39 CAVENDISH SQUARE.

(*Three months pass.*)

ACT II

SCENE—SAINT EDANA'S WELL AND CHURCH, FONTLEAS.

(*Six months pass.*)

ACT III

SCENE—THE ABBOT'S KITCHEN, FONTLEAS.

(*Nine months pass.*)

ACT IV

SCENE—THE VICARAGE DRAWING-ROOM, FONTLEAS.

Time.—PRESENT DAY.

The following is a copy of the original play-bill of
" The Physician."

CRITERION THEATRE.

Lessee and Manager—Mr. Charles Wyndham.

On Thursday, 25th March 1897, for the first time,
A new Play of modern life, in Four Acts, entitled

THE PHYSICIAN

By HENRY ARTHUR JONES

Dr. Lewin Carey .	Mr. Charles Wyndham.
Rev. Peregrine Hinde	Mr. Alfred Bishop.
Walter Amphiel	Mr. T. B. Thalberg.
Dr. Brooker	Mr. Leslie Kenyon.
Stephen Gurdon	Mr. J. G. Taylor.
James Hebbings	Mr. Kenneth Douglas.
John Dibley	Mr. A. E. George.
Viccars .	Mr. F. H. Tyler.
Postman . .	Mr. F. Vigay.
Lady Valerie Camville .	Miss Marion Terry.
Mrs. Bowden .	Miss E. Vining.
Mrs. Dibley	Miss Carlotta Addison.
Louisa Pack	Miss Jocelyn.
Marah	Miss Valli Valli.
Lizzie . .	Miss M. Clayton.
Saunders . .	Miss D. Fellowes.
Edana Hinde	Miss Mary Moore.

ACT I

Consulting-Room at Dr. Lewin Carey's,
39 Cavendish Square.

(Three months pass.)

ACT II

SAINT EDANA'S WELL AND CHURCH AT FONTLEAS
(Walter Hann).

(*Six months pass.*)

ACT III

THE ABBOT'S KITCHEN, FONTLEAS (Walter Hann).

(*Ten months pass.*)

ACT IV

THE VICARAGE, FONTLEAS.

Time.—THE PRESENT.

There will be an interval of about ten minutes between Acts I., II.,
III., and about five minutes between Acts III. and IV.

Matinees of "The Physician," Wednesday, 31st March,
Saturday, 3rd April, and every following Saturday.

Stage Manager—Mr. PERCY HUTCHISON.
Musical Director—Mr. VICTOR HOLLAENDER.
Acting Manager and Treasurer—Mr. E. HARVEY.

ACT I

SCENE—CONSULTING-ROOM AT DR. LEWIN CAREY'S, CAVENDISH SQUARE, A SUBSTANTIALLY FURNISHED ROOM, SUCH AS WOULD BE USED BY A LONDON PHYSICIAN IN GOOD PRACTICE.

Door down stage L. *Door at back* L. *Fireplace at back* R. *Windows* R. *Book-cases, containing medical works, round the room. One or two good oil paintings.*

TIME: *late on an April afternoon.*

Enter door at back, VICCARS, DR. CAREY'S *butler, showing in* WALTER AMPHIEL. AMPHIEL *is a pale, thin, and very delicate-looking man about thirty ; striking, earnest features, with a winning, lovable expression ; rather weak mouth ; restless, furtive eyes with a hunted look in them. His ordinary manner is absent, dreamy, self-absorbed, and there is a strangeness and indecision in his movements and speech, but this at times gives place to fits of feverish energy.*

B

VICCARS. Dr. Carey is attending a consultation, sir, but I expect him back shortly.

AMPHIEL. I'll wait.

VICCARS. What name shall I say?

AMPHIEL. My name doesn't matter. I'll wait.

(*Exit* VICCARS *at back.*)

(AMPHIEL *furtively watches* VICCARS *off, and as soon as the door has closed, goes quickly to the book-shelves, runs his eye eagerly over them as if searching for something, takes out a particular book, looks at index, opens it at a certain page, sits down, reads eagerly. A short pause.*)

Enter VICCARS *at back, showing in* DR. BROOKER, *a middle-aged man, brisk, genial, robust: sanguine complexion; a little stout, a little bald.*

(*As* BROOKER *enters,* AMPHIEL *shows recognition and a little embarrassment, hiding his head behind his book.*)

BROOKER (*entering*). Thank you, Viccars. Dr. Carey does expect me, doesn't he?

VICCARS. Yes, sir. He left word if you came that he'd be back almost at once. Shall I get you anything after your journey, sir?

BROOKER. No, thank you. Well, just a cup of tea, if you'll be so good. (*Exit* VICCARS *at back.*)

BROOKER (*sitting down, catches sight of* AMPHIEL'S *face as he looks up furtively from his book*). I beg pardon, my name is Brooker—Dr. Brooker of Folkestone. I've had the pleasure of meeting you somewhere?

AMPHIEL (*with slight embarrassment*). I think not —I don't remember you.

BROOKER (*still looking at him*). I suppose I was mistaken. Your face seemed familiar to me.

(A little pause.)

AMPHIEL. Very interesting place, a doctor's consulting-room?

BROOKER. H'm!—not very—to the doctor.

AMPHIEL. This room, for instance. How many strange stories and confessions these walls must have listened to! How many men and women must have entered that door with hope in their hearts, and received their death sentence, sitting perhaps where I am sitting now!

BROOKER. Oh, don't speak of us as if we were bloodthirsty hanging judges. Say rather how many men have entered that door with despair in their hearts and gone out cheered and comforted!

AMPHIEL. Dr. Carey is marvellously skilful in certain—certain nervous diseases, isn't he?

BROOKER. He's marvellously skilful in all kinds of diseases. He has made a great reputation with nerve diseases, simply because this is a nervous age. Everybody is suffering from neurasthenia to-day. Except myself, thank God!

VICCARS *re-enters* L. *with tea on salver, which he brings to* DR. BROOKER. AMPHIEL *puts book on table, open.*

BROOKER (*looking steadily at* AMPHIEL). Surely I —didn't you consult me one Sunday evening three or four years ago?

AMPHIEL. No, no, I've never met you. (*To* VICCARS.) Dr. Carey hasn't returned.' (*Takes out watch.*) I'll call again by and by.

(*Exit* AMPHIEL *at back rather hurriedly.*)

VICCARS (*at door, looking after him, calling off*). The door, Thomas.

(*Meantime* BROOKER *has taken up the book which* AMPHIEL *has put down. He looks at the page, raises his eyebrows, puts book on table again, leaving it open.*)

BROOKER (*taking tea*). And how have you been all this time, Viccars?

VICCARS. I've kept pretty tolerable, I thank you, sir.

BROOKER. And Dr. Carey?

VICCARS. About as usual, sir.

BROOKER. He wrote me rather an urgent letter. I thought perhaps something was wrong. (VICCARS *does not reply. There is a short pause.*) He has had no trouble, no misfortune, no loss?

VICCARS. No, sir. At least, none that it's any business of mine to take notice of.

BROOKER. You're right, Viccars. Of course, I

didn't wish you to speak of Dr. Carey's affairs. He's quite well?

VICCARS. In body, I believe, quite well, sir. Though, of course, the journey to Egypt and his attendance on the Pasha have fagged him a good deal.

BROOKER. You went with him, Viccars?

VICCARS. Yes, sir. I had that honour. Dr. Carey waited on the Pasha night and day, and I waited on Dr. Carey. It was wonderful to watch him.

BROOKER. How—wonderful?

VICCARS. He seemed determined to keep the life in the old fellow. I don't know what it is about Dr. Carey, but he seems to have got that in him—well, I can't describe it—but if once Dr. Carey makes up his mind that a certain patient shall live, it seems more than that patient dare do to die, and it's more than Death dare do to lay hands on him.

BROOKER. And Death did not lay hands on the Pasha?

VICCARS. No, sir. We pulled the old chap through and left him happy, and comparatively rollicking, so to speak, with his four wives. I think I heard the carriage. (*Looking out of window.*) Yes, here is Dr. Carey. (*Crossing to door at back.*)

VICCARS *opens door.* DR. CAREY *enters.*

(*Exit* VICCARS.)

(DR. LEWIN CAREY *is a man of from forty-five to fifty. He has a strong intellectual*

*face ; sensitive mobile features, with fre-
quently changing play of humour and
melancholy ; kind penetrating eyes ; a
tender caressing voice ; calm, restrained,
professional manner. He comes very
affectionately to* BROOKER, *takes his
hand, holds it some moments without
speaking.*)

DR. C.   My dear fellow, I knew you'd come.

BROOKER.   Why, of course.   I didn't understand
your letter.

DR. C.   I want to consult you about myself.

(BROOKER *looks astonished.*   DR. CAREY
*motions him to a seat.   During the
following scene* BROOKER *is seated.   DR.
CAREY *sometimes sits, sometimes stands,
sometimes walks about.*)

BROOKER.   What's the matter?

DR. C.   Everything.   Nothing.   You'll call it
neurasthenia, and you'll give me some placebo, which
I shan't believe in, and which I shan't take.

BROOKER.   But I'm only a country practitioner.
The best man for nerves is Lewin Carey, 39 Cavendish
Square.   Why don't you go to him?

DR. C.   I have, but he only laughs at me and
says : " Physician, heal thyself."   That's the one
thing that rings constantly in my ears day and night,
" Physician, heal thyself!   Physician, heal thyself."
I can't, Brooker.

BROOKER. Go on. Tell me all.

DR. C. My dear old fellow, have patience with me! The last fifteen years, while you've been comfortably ploughing and whistling on your way amongst rural measles and accouchements, I've stood here an open receptacle for all the nervous diseases of the age to be poured into. And the mischief is, Brooker, I'm so sympathetic, I've caught them all.

BROOKER. You're a little overworked.

DR. C. No, it's not that. I'm just at the prime of life with a splendid constitution. I'm getting to the top of my profession, I'm richer than my needs, I'm honoured, fêted, envied—and yet, by God, Brooker, I don't believe there's in any London slum, or jail, or workhouse, a poor wretch with such a horrible despair in his heart as I have to-day.

BROOKER. You know the causes of nervous breakdown. What past excess is calling on you for payment?

DR. C. My youth was pretty much about the average. I don't pretend to justify it. I don't pretend to regret it. If any past excess is calling on me for payment now, it's excess of work rather than excess of pleasure.

BROOKER. And since your youth? (*Pause.*) Is there any woman in this business, Carey?

DR. C. I've had an attachment for some years past. I won't tell you her name, though you can easily learn it if you care to inquire. Seven years ago

I met one of the most beautiful women in London. She had married a blackguard, who neglected her. And certainly she had as much excuse as ever a woman had for forming other ties. Her husband has lived abroad for years, and practically doesn't exist. I go out very little, as you know, but she goes a great deal into society.

BROOKER.   And what has society said to this?

DR. C.   Society, with its perfect good-nature, its perfect tact and sympathy with a genuine attachment such as ours, has nodded and smiled, and whispered no doubt, but has never *openly* said one word against her.

BROOKER.   This attachment—does it continue?

DR. C.   No.   For some time I have felt that she has cared for me less and less.   When I came back from Egypt a month ago I found a letter from her, breaking it off.

BROOKER.   And you've not seen her?

DR. C.   No, she's travelling abroad.   I've written to her several times begging her to return, but she hasn't replied.

BROOKER.   And so you're steadily breaking your heart for this woman?

DR. C.   I miss her terribly—hourly.   She was such a delightful companion.   But though I've loved her deeply, and she has loved me—after a fashion—I've never rested in her love.   I've always known her to be a coquette—a flaming, intellectual coquette—

whose very attractions make it impossible for her to be constant. Good God, Brooker! are any of us constant to anybody, or to anything, or to ourselves —even our worst selves? Don't let me maunder any more about her. *She* isn't the matter with me—or if she is, she's not *all* the matter with me. I go deeper than that.

BROOKER.   What is the matter with you?

DR. C.   I tell you I've caught the disease of our time, of our society, of our civilisation.

BROOKER.   What's that?

DR. C.   Middle age. Disillusionment. My youth's gone. My beliefs are gone. I enjoy nothing. I believe in nothing.

BROOKER.   There's no cure for lost youth, I'm afraid. But for lost belief——

DR. C.   The cure for that is to turn churchwarden and go round with the plate on Sundays, I suppose.

BROOKER.   Don't sneer at us poor fools who do still believe in something.

DR. C.   Sneer at you! I envy you. Belief! That's the placebo I want. That would cure me.

BROOKER.   Don't you believe in your work?

DR. C.   My work means nothing to me. Success means nothing to me. I cure people with a grin and a sneer. I keep on asking myself, "To what end? To what end?"

BROOKER.   Come and dress, let's get an early dinner and go to a music hall.

DR. C.   That's your placebo, is it?

BROOKER.   Surely, Carey, you must know there's nothing the matter with you.

DR. C.   Don't I tell you there's nothing the matter with me, and that I can endure it no longer.   Brooker, my practice is a very valuable one.   I want you to take it up and carry it on.

BROOKER.   You're not in earnest?

DR. C.   Indeed I am.   We'll talk it over at dinner. Don't argue with me, I've made up my mind.

BROOKER.   And you—what will you do?

DR. C.   I don't know.

BROOKER.   Where will you go?

DR. C.   I don't know.

BROOKER.   Surely you have some plan?

DR. C.   None in this world, except to walk out of that door and let it clang for ever on my present self. I want a new impulse, a new outlook on life—no, I want a new life itself.   I may go to India.   I'm interested in these cholera experiments.

BROOKER.   To what end?

DR. C.   Ah, to what end?   To save life.   To what end?   I can't tell you.   But I've still got the healing instinct strong within me in spite of what I've told you; if any poor devil suffering from some mortal disease were to come in at that door and ask me to help him, I should fling myself heart and soul into his case and fight like a tiger to pull him through. And all the time my grinning, sneering, second self

would be standing beside me and asking me "To
what end? To what end?" (*With a gesture of
weariness and despair.*) Let me get out of this,
Brooker. Come in as soon as you can and set me
free.

Enter VICCARS *at back, with lady's visiting card on
tray, which he brings to* DR. CAREY. DR. CAREY
takes card, shows great delight.

VICCARS. Lady is waiting in the next room, sir.
(*Going off at back.*)

DR. C. (*in a low tone to* BROOKER, *showing great
feeling*). It's she. She has come back to me !

BROOKER. I've a letter or two to write. Perhaps
Viccars will show me to my room.

VICCARS (*at door at back*). This way, sir. (*Exit.*)

DR. C. (*with great feeling*). I was wrong, Brooker.
I care for her more than I know. It's her absence
that has ailed me. I shall be well now.

(BROOKER *wrings* CAREY'S *hand with great
cordiality, and exit at back.* DR.
CAREY *goes to door* L., *opens it.*)

DR. C. Val !

Enter door at back LADY VALERIE CAMVILLE, *a handsome woman about thirty-three ; bright red hair,
large brown eyes with a merry twinkle ; high fore-
head ; rather large mouth with great expression ; a*

*face with beauty, intellectuality, and humour, with-
out spirituality. DR. CAREY goes to her with the
utmost tenderness and respect, kisses her hand softly
two or three times, then holds it tenderly, looking
at her with great affection.*

DR. C.   You got my letters?

LADY V.   Yes.   (*Withdraws her hand.*)   You
begged me at least to see you and say "Good-bye."
Your last letter was so piteous, I couldn't help coming.
(*Holding out hand in the frankest way.*)   Good-bye.

DR. C. (*cut to the quick*).   You've not come to
say that?   (*Doesn't take her hand.*)

LADY V.   Indeed I have.   If you remember we
made a compact at the beginning of our friendship——

DR. C.   Our friendship!   We were friends, were
we not?

LADY V.   We were very good friends indeed, and
we very sensibly agreed that the moment we began to
feel the least little bit tired of each other, the moment
boredom supervened, we would have the courage to
own the truth and—part.

(*Again offering hand, which he doesn't take.*)

DR. C. (*piteously*).   Are you tired of me, Val?

LADY V.   Not at the present moment.   Altogether,
I think you bear the test of constant companionship
better than most men would.   (*Smiling at him.*)   Still,
my dear Lewin, don't let us blink the horrible fact

that boredom has supervened.   That Sunday at Henley last year!

DR. C.   Oh, a wet English Sunday!

LADY V.   No amount of British climate or British Sunday can excuse a man for treating a woman as if she had been married to him for a dozen years! Besides, boredom has supervened on other occasions.

DR. C. (*jealously*).   Val—you've not—you've not met any one else?

LADY V.   Ah! you shouldn't ask me that!

DR. C.   Why not?

LADY V.   Because you know I should tell the biggest of big fibs, rather than give you pain.

DR. C.   Then you have?

LADY V.   No.   I've only thought matters over. (*Again offering hand.*)   Good-bye.

DR. C.   I can't say it.   What reason is there for us to part?

LADY V.   Our friendship must end some day and somehow.   Think.   How would you wish it to end? In a yawn?   In a squabble?   In a scandal?

DR. C.   I should wish it to end in—death.

LADY V.   Would you?   Now that's the very last way in which I should wish it to end.   At least, if it's my death you mean.

DR. C.   Why not the scandal?

LADY V. (*looks at him questioningly*).   You'd be obliged to marry me!

DR. C.   Obliged?   Dare you face it?

LADY V. Gracious, no! To sink into social extinction in a bog of newspaper mud! No, trust me, this is our fine artistic moment for bidding each other adieu. We part with the pleasantest memories of the past, with the best wishes for the future, and with just the merest shade of regret (*looks at him roguishly, sighs*); at least, on my side.

DR. C. On your side there will be the merest shade of regret. On my side there will be despair.

LADY V. And so there should be! Anything less than despair for some months, or at least weeks, would be uncomplimentary to me.

DR. C. (*coming to her passionately*). Val, don't torture me! I can't let you go. (*About to clasp her.*)

LADY V. (*shaking her head, warning him off with her forefinger*). I leave for Scotland to-night.

DR. C. Scotland! What for?

LADY V. To escape boredom. I see it still hovering, ready to close impenetrably round us the moment we take up our old lives.

DR. C. Why should we take up our old lives? Val, take up a new life with me from to-day—from this moment.

LADY V. New life! How? Where?

DR. C. Anywhere! I'm leaving London, giving up my practice——

LADY V. My dear Lewin, what strange freak is this?

DR. C. It's no freak. If I stay in London I shall

come to some miserable end. I shall either go mad, or commit suicide, or become a fashionable London physician. I don't want to do either. I've got thirty good years of life in front of me.

LADY V. And how do you propose to spend them?

DR. C. In work. In duty.

LADY V. Duty? H'm! That's some article for the consumption of the great middle classes, isn't it? Like the things they get at Whiteley's and the Stores. I'm sure it isn't for the elect—for you and me. What work? What duty?

DR. C. I should like to go to India and thoroughly work out these cholera experiments.

LADY V. And to boredom add ghastliness. I don't want to go microbe-hunting in India. I like big game.

DR. C. Very well. We'll travel, go where you please, do what you please. Only (*very piteously*) don't leave me, Val. These last few weeks since you've been away I've had a horrible time. I couldn't tell what ailed me. When I knew that you had come back, my heart began to beat again. My hand trembled when I took your card just now, and when you came into the room, didn't you see, I could scarcely speak for joy?

LADY V. (*a little touched*). My poor Lewin, I didn't know you cared so much for me.

DR. C. I didn't know it myself till I had lost you.

Val, come back to me. I cling to you! You are all
I have in the world! Take me, do what you please
with me! Make me at least believe in you! What
is it you want? Is it love? I'll give you all I have
to the last drain of my heart. Is it marriage? I'll
face the disgrace with you, shelter you from it so far
as I can. Val, I offer you my heart and my name
with all the respect and worship of my nature. (*Long
pause.*) What do you say?   .

> (*She has listened with great attention and is a
> little moved by his passionate pleading,
> stands as if undecided, then looks at him
> pityingly, sighs, speaks in a firm matter-
> of-fact, but not unkind tone.*)

LADY V.   I'm very sorry.   But it must be adieu—
and now.

DR. C.   Don't leave me, Val.

LADY V.   I must be in Scotland to-morrow morning, and I must catch the train.

DR. C.   Don't leave me, Val.

LADY V.   What a heavenly attitude of melancholy
you have!

DR. C.   Don't leave me, Val.

LADY V.   Alas, poor dear! I must! (*Blows him
a kiss.*)   Good-bye.   (*Exit L.*)

> (*She closes the door after her. He stands,
> looks after her, his hands tightly clasped
> in front of him ; his features hardening,
> his eyes fixed, his whole attitude one of*

great mental anguish changing into despair. A long pause. VICCARS *slowly
and timidly opens door at back and
looks in.*)

VICCARS. Are you engaged, sir?

DR. C. (*relaxing his strained attitude with an effort,
speaking in an intensely calm tone*). No. What is it?

VICCARS (*enters, brings in card on salver*). A
young lady says she appointed to meet her father here
at half-past five. He hasn't come, and she wishes to
know if you could see her for a few minutes.

DR. C. Show her in.

∴   (VICCARS *goes, leaves door open.* DR. CAREY
*walks listlessly across the room. Re-
enter* VICCARS, *at back, showing in*
EDANA HINDE, *a bright, eager girl, not
quite twenty, prettily dressed, but a little
countrified.*)

VICCARS. Miss Hinde. (*Exit* VICCARS.)

EDANA. I'm so sorry to trouble you. My father
arranged to meet me here, but he has gone to some
old bookshops, and I daresay he has forgotten all
about me.

DR. C. Will you be seated? (*She sits.*) What
can I do for you?

EDANA. I hardly know how to tell you. You
won't think it very strange of me—I wanted to ask
you about somebody else—— (*A pause.*)

DR. C. Go on.

C

EDANA (*a little embarrassed*). His life is so valuable. You must have heard his name—Mr. Walter Amphiel.

DR. C. Amphiel? Amphiel? Oh yes, the man who is making all this stir about the temperance question.

EDANA. He is giving his life to it.

DR. C. He is a friend of yours?

EDANA. Yes. (*Pause.*) I am to be his wife.

DR. C. And you wish——?

EDANA. He gives himself to the work night and day. He is killing himself for others.

DR. C. Then he is unjust to himself and to you.

EDANA. Oh, it doesn't matter for me. But I want his life to be spared.

DR. C. And you wish me to see him and persuade him to give it up?

EDANA. Oh no, he wouldn't give up the work! And I wouldn't have him! We have both put our hands to the plough. And (*very glowingly*) I wish nothing better for either of us than to die for our cause if need were. (*He is looking at her with interest and a little astonishment.*) I beg pardon, you don't understand me.

DR. C. I don't quite understand what you wish me to do.

EDANA. I want you to see him and advise him how to take care of his health.

DR. C. Certainly. Send him to me to-morrow morning.

EDANA. He won't come. He has a great dislike to seeing doctors, and when I beg him he only smiles at me, and says he shall live long enough. But I can see such a change in him the last few months. He grows paler and thinner, and more careworn. Couldn't you come to him?

DR. C. Where?

EDANA. We live at Fontleas, near Buxenham.

DR. C. Is he there now?

EDANA. No. He is passing though London to-day on his way to the Temperance Congress at Southampton to-morrow. Couldn't you come to Fontleas, unknown to him, and stay a day or two and watch him, and find out all about him, and tell me what to do?

DR. C. It would be very unusual.

EDANA. Would it be impossible?

DR. C. You are very much concerned for him.

EDANA. Oh, I can't tell you how much! He is so good, and gentle, and unselfish! He came into a large fortune last year. He is giving it all away to the cause. Isn't it great of him to give up everything for others?

DR. C. What made you come to me?

EDANA. We've been reading about your journey to Egypt and how you saved the Pasha's life. Yours must be splendid work, too! I've often thought that if I were a man I should like to be a doctor. (*She sees* DR. CAREY *is watching her, stops suddenly, confused.*) I beg your pardon. Could you come to Fontleas?

DR. C. Certainly I could come. I come to Buxenham occasionally. I send some of my patients there for the waters. By the way, isn't there a well or a spring at Fontleas?

EDANA. Yes, a holy well. You've heard of it?

DR. C. I think I have. Saint—Saint——

EDANA. Saint Edana's well. It had great healing properties in the middle ages. Pilgrims used to come there from all parts, and thousands were cured by drinking its waters.

DR. C. In the middle ages. And now they have come to me.

EDANA. Oh, we've had some cures in this century.

DR. C. Indeed.

EDANA. My father is Vicar of Fontleas, and he's writing a life of Saint Edana.

DR. C. Saint Edana! It's an uncommon name.

EDANA. I was named after her.

DR. C. Saint Edana! It's a pretty name.

(*A pause.*)

EDANA (*rising*). I'm taking up your valuable time——

DR. C. When will Mr. Amphiel be at Fontleas?

EDANA. He lives there. But he's often away for

weeks together on temperance work. I could let you know. Will you come and see him?

DR. C. If there is anything I can do——

EDANA. Then you will come! How kind of you! But I'm sure when you know him you'll think his life worth all your care.

DR. C. If he is dear to you I'm sure it must be.

Enter VICCARS *at back, showing in the* REVEREND *'PEREGRINE* HINDE, *a very quaint old country clergyman, rather over sixty, with very bright eyes, pleasant features, indicating a mixture of shrewdness and simplicity. He has a habit of humming little snatches of sacred tunes to himself, and punctuates nearly every sentence with a hearty little chuckle at his own small wit. He carries two or three large old volumes under his arm.*

VICCARS (*announcing*). Mr. Hinde.

(*Exit* VICCARS.)

REV. P. (*comes up to* DR. CAREY, *humming a little snatch, leaves off abruptly*). Dr. Carey? (DR. CAREY *bows.*) I've been with the saints all the afternoon. (*Tapping the books under his arm.*) And in their society I forgot all about you. I hope you'll excuse me.

DR. C. Certainly. From the little I know of the saints I'm sure they must be far more agreeable company than I am.

REV. P. Not more agreeable, but say more profitable—for a man of my age. You see, I may have to meet them in a few years, and I shouldn't like not to feel quite at home amongst them. (*Chuckles and hums.*)   Now, Edana, what is to be done about Walter?

EDANA.   Dr. Carey has promised to come to Fontleas to see him.

REV. P.   The poor boy is working himself to death in the cause of temperance.   Dear me, how very intemperate all these good temperance folks are, aren't they?   Still, it's a good cause—a sacred cause.   I used to take my glass of wine and I used to enjoy it. Walter has persuaded me to give it up.   I miss it (*regretfully*), still it's a good cause—a sacred cause. And may I ask what your fee will be for coming to Fontleas, Dr. Carey?

DR. C.   Oh, don't trouble about that, Mr Hinde.

REV. P.   Oh, but I must.   I'm not rich.   My stipend for doctoring men's souls is two hundred and forty pounds per annum, or thirteen shillings a day.   I hope you don't consider doctoring men's bodies is worth more than (*a little hum*) say ten times as much as doctoring their souls?

DR. C.   That all depends upon the doctor.   I'll come to Fontleas and see Mr. Amphiel.   But we won't say anything about the fee till I've done my work.   Is there any place at Fontleas where I can stay?

REV. P.   We can offer you the hospitality of the Vicarage.

DR. C.   You're very kind, but I'm going to take

a long rest from my practice, and I might possibly stay some considerable time.   Is there a comfortable inn?

REV. P.   I'm afraid there isn't.   We are all such staunch temperance folks at Fontleas that we feel bound to make people who drink as uncomfortable as we can, don't we, Edana?   (*Chuckles.*)

EDANA.   There's Granny Barton's.   She has one or two very large comfortable rooms.

DR. C.   What is her address?

EDANA.   The Abbot's Kitchen, Fontleas.

DR. C.   The Abbot's Kitchen?

REV. P.   It was the Abbot's Kitchen, but there being no further use for abbots, and no further use for good living in Fontleas, it was turned into a farmhouse.   And now there being no further use in England for farms and farmhouses, the poor old creature has sold her land and lets her rooms to visitors from Buxenham.

EDANA.   She's a dear old soul.

REV. P.   And she so far sustains the traditions of the spot that she can cook a very good dinner.

DR. C. (*making a note*).   The Abbot's Kitchen. Very well.   I'll come to Fontleas as soon as I can get away from London.

> (*The* REV. PEREGRINE HINDE *takes up his books.* EDANA *picks up the book which* AMPHIEL *has left, glances at the title, shows interest, looks at it during the following conversation.*)

DR. C. (*touching the books which the* REV. PERE-
GRINE HINDE *is taking up*). Your lore is very different
from mine.

REV. P.   Yes, so much more interesting.

DR. C.   Why?

REV. P.   Don't you think men's souls are more
interesting than their bodies?

DR. C.   I never saw a man's soul.

REV. P.   I never saw a mother's love, but I'm sure
it's about the realest thing on this side of the grave.

EDANA (*who has been looking at the book*).   How
very curious!

DR. C.   What?

EDANA.   This book on Alcoholic Mania.

DR. C.   Yes, it's interesting.   But the author
rides his theory that drunkenness is a disease a little
too hard.   (*Edana continues reading.*)   Miss Hinde
tells me you are writing a life of Saint Edana.

REV. P.   Yes, it's very puzzling.   One history
recounts that she went to Cornwall and died there at
the age of twenty, the most glorious visions being
vouchsafed to all around her as her spirit passed away.

DR. C.   Ah!   I've been to Cornwall——

REV. P.   But you saw no visions?   No, it's a rare
faculty, and it seems to be growing rarer.   We who
have it are highly favoured.   (*Chuckles and hums.*)
Another account says that as Saint Edana was crossing to Ireland at the age of fifty, the ship was over-
taken in a storm.   And while the mariners cursed

and blasphemed, she prayed that her life alone might be taken and all the others spared to repent. And so it was.

DR. C. And another history recounts——?

REV. P. That she died full of good works at the age of ninety on the spot where my vicarage now stands.

DR. C. And which history do you believe?

REV. P. All three. (*Hums and chuckles.*) You see, so many people nowadays believe in nothing at all, it does no harm to have a few old-fashioned folks like myself, who believe a great deal too much, believe everything that's told them—so long as it's beautiful and helpful! Good-bye, Dr. Carey. Come, Edana!

> (*Exit at back, humming and chuckling, his books under his arm.*)

EDANA (*puts down book*). Then we shall see you at Fontleas?

DR. C. In about a week. (*Shaking hands.*)

EDANA. Thank you! Thank you! Oh, if you can give him health and strength——

> (*Her eyes fill with tears. Exit at back hurriedly. DR. CAREY stands looking after her for some moments as if deeply interested; comes down stage.*)

BROOKER *enters at the open door.*

DR. C. Brooker, make haste and come into my practice. I want to get away.

BROOKER. Where?

DR. C. Did you see that girl who went out? Her lover is ill—dying, she says. She wants me to come and see him.

BROOKER. And you're going?

DR. C. Why not? Why not there as well as anywhere? Why not that as well as anything else?

BROOKER. You mean to give up this splendid practice, your position, your career——

DR. C. I tell you I can't stay here, especially after to-day. Besides, this man Amphiel has a great mission.

BROOKER. Mission?

DR. C. He's this Walter Amphiel, the man who is organising the temperance movement.

BROOKER. And do you agree with that kind of fanaticism?

DR. C. Is it fanaticism? The girl's face glowed like a live coal when she spoke of her cause and her lover. How she loves the fellow! Brooker, it's better to be a fanatic than a cynic.

BROOKER. It's better still to be neither. It's better to be a good common-sense citizen and pay your rates and taxes.

DR. C. No, it isn't. Good common-sense citizens when they die—well, they think they go to heaven or hell, but they only go to limbo—and I should like to go to heaven *or* hell; the latter for preference, I think, because it's only when we suffer, as I'm suffering now, that we can make sure that we're alive. By the way, did you take down that book of Fuller's on Alcoholic Mania? (*Pointing to book on table.*)

BROOKER. No, I found a young fellow here reading it. I thought I remembered his face—in fact, I'm sure I did. He came to me some three or four years ago. He puzzled me. I fancied at the time, from a hint that he dropped, that he'd been drinking heavily.

Re-enter VICCARS *at back.*

VICCARS. A gentleman to consult you, sir. He won't give his name.

DR. C. Show him in. (*Exit* VICCARS *at back.*)

BROOKER (*taking out watch*). It's almost time to dress for dinner. You said nothing more about——

DR. C. She only came to say "good-bye." She has said it. (*A very bitter laugh.*) Brooker, I'll come with you to a music hall to-night.

Re-enter VICCARS, L., *showing in* WALTER AMPHIEL, *who meets* BROOKER *as he is going out.* AMPHIEL *again shows slight recognition, and avoids looking at* BROOKER. BROOKER *bows slightly.*)
(*Exit* BROOKER *and* VICCARS *at back.*)

AMPHIEL. Dr. Carey, I've come on a curious errand.

(DR. CAREY *points to a chair, looks rather*

fixedly at AMPHIEL, *who remains stand-*
ing with a somewhat embarrassed, shifty
manner. DR. CAREY *again points to*
chair. AMPHIEL *sits.* DR. CAREY *sits.*)

DR. C.   What can I do for you?

AMPHIEL.   Nothing for myself.   I'm in excellent
health, as you can see.   (*With a smile.*)

DR. C.   Go on.

AMPHIEL.   I've come to ask your advice about a
very dear friend of mine—almost my brother.   I've
been staying with him lately, and to my horror I
discovered that he gives way to periodical fits of
drunkenness.   I tried to persuade him to come to
you, but he was ashamed.   I want you to advise me
about him.

DR. C.   I couldn't advise you without seeing
him.   I don't know his constitution or how far it
is impaired.

AMPHIEL.   Oh, I don't think there is any serious
damage done.   And I want you to give me some
general rules for his guidance.   Drunkenness is really
a disease, isn't it?

DR. C.   All vice is disease.   All evil habits are
the exact expression of some physical derangement.
An evil thought signifies that the brain is to that
extent disordered, the same as an attack of indiges-
tion signifies that the stomach is to that extent disordered.

AMPHIEL.   But we can't help our thoughts!   My

friend can't help these fits of drunkenness. I'm sure
he can't! Surely you can advise me what he ought
to do?

DR. C. How often do these outbreaks occur?

AMPHIEL. Sometimes every month or two—sometimes he manages to control himself for three or four
months. Then suddenly he tells me he has this
irresistible craving for drink—it's so overwhelming that
he'd lie, or steal, or murder almost to get it. Then
he goes away, he tells me, hides from his friends, and
gives way to drink and—other dissipation—at least,
so I gathered. When the fit is over he spends a few
awful days in anguish and remorse, and then, when
he is sufficiently recovered, he goes back to his home.

DR. C. And nobody suspects him?

AMPHIEL. Nobody. Except myself. And I only
found it out by the merest accident.

DR. C. What is his age?

AMPHIEL (*slight hesitation*). Thirty-one.

DR. C. How long has he been subject to these
outbreaks?

AMPHIEL. About five or six years.

DR. C. Did they come on gradually from constant and little drinking? Or did they begin after
some one definite cause, such as an illness, a shock,
a bereavement, or an accident? How did they
originate?

AMPHIEL (*after a longish pause*). He told me all.
He ruined a girl near to his home. She brought his

child to her father and then left her home again, went from worse to worse, and drifted away nobody knows where. Her mother died from the shame and grief and my friend drank to drown his remorse. Ever since then, at intervals, he has had these outbreaks.

DR. C. What is his occupation?

AMPHIEL (*hesitates*). He—he——

DR. C. (*rising*). You had better send your friend to some good physician.

AMPHIEL (*rising*). But can't you tell me what to do with him? Would a voyage to India benefit him?

DR. C. I couldn't say. Send him to some good physician. What is he afraid of? A physician knows nothing of shame. Any one part of this wonderful machine that gets out of order is just the same as another to him. His only care is to heal. Come, now (*with great kindness and inviting* AMPHIEL'S *confidence*), if it were yourself, I'm sure you wouldn't hesitate to trust me?

(AMPHIEL *responds with a movement towards* DR. CAREY *as if about to give* DR. CAREY *all his confidence, then suddenly checks himself and shows some embarrassment.*)

AMPHIEL. My friend is in a position of great responsibility. I mustn't betray him without first consulting him. (*Takes out purse.*) The fee?

DR. C. There is no fee.

AMPHIEL. But I——

DR. C. There is no fee till I have advised your friend. Good-day, Mr.—I didn't catch your name——

AMPHIEL. Mr.—a—Williams.

DR. C. Mr.—a—Williams.   (*Rings bell.*)

AMPHIEL (*going, turns*). It is a disease, isn't it? I may tell him that? He can't help these outbreaks?

DR. C. (*dryly, coldly, a little grimly*). Certainly it is a disease. But don't let your friend lay the flattering unction to his soul that he can't help it, for that means his ruin. It is a disease, and the worse he has it the more he *must* help it. Has he a wife?

AMPHIEL. No. But he's engaged to the dearest, most innocent girl—that's the madness of it for him.

DR. C. It may one day be the madness of it for her. Won't the thought of her save him?

AMPHIEL. It has kept him from the worst—at times.

DR. C. (*very significantly*). Let it keep him from the worst—always. (VICCARS *appears at door at back.*) The door, Viccars.

> (*Exit* VICCARS. AMPHIEL *goes out slowly, irresolutely, troubled; looks back at* DR. CAREY *as he goes off.* DOCTOR *stands looking after him.*)

Rather slow Curtain.

(*Three months pass between Acts I. and II.*)

GROUND PLAN OF ACT II.

Landscape back cloth

Gate

Door

Leper's window

L.

Wall

Slab

Pool

Weeping willow

Low wall 2 ft. high

Gate

Steps

Wall

Seat

Tree trunk

Gravel walk

R.

ACT II

*The churchyard wall, an irregular crumbling mass of
weatherbeaten stone and brick, runs across the stage
diagonally, from down stage* R. *to up stage* L. *A
large carved slab of stone in the wall forms the back
of the well, which is in the centre of the stage; the
water running from the slab forms a pool which is
surrounded by a low thick wall of crumbling masonry
about two feet high and very thick. A weeping
willow springs from the pool and hangs over the
well. On the slab is carved the inscription in letters
which are worn and scarcely decipherable, " Whosoever drinketh of this water shall thirst again, but
whosoever drinketh of the water that I shall give
him shall never thirst." There is a wicket gate in
the wall at back just to* R. *of well, and another
wicket gate at extreme corner* L., *both of these giving
glimpses of landscape in evening light. A few steps
lead up to the wicket gate* R. *Down stage* R. *the*

D

*trunk of an old elm tree with a seat running round
it. On the L. of the stage going up to the corner
wicket gate is the Church of St. Edana, a very
simple Early English building with a low roof and
covered with ivy. In the church a small door, and
a small window, formerly the lepers' window, such
as is seen in many old churches.*

TIME: *a summer Sunday evening.*

Discover DR. CAREY *and* EDANA *seated on the well.*
EDANA *is in a dress of soft white muslin.*

DR. C.   And it was at this well that Saint Edana
worked her most wonderful cures.   What diseases
did she treat?

EDANA.   All kinds of diseases.

DR. C.   Like a patent medicine.

EDANA.   Yes—and like Nature.

DR. C.   Nature's a sad bungler.

EDANA.   No! No!

DR. C.   Yes! Yes! She's terribly careless and
terribly cruel.

EDANA.   No! No! I won't have you slander
your mother.

DR. C.   Tell me some more about Saint Edana.

EDANA.   She is said to have cured many lepers.
You see that little round window?   That was the
lepers' window in the old time.   They weren't allowed
to mix with the congregation, and so they used to
come there and join in the services from outside.

Dr. C. The lepers' window! That was my window.

Edana. Yes, I saw you looking through it this morning. Are you coming to church this evening?

Dr. C. No. I feel my right place is outside— with the lepers.

Edana. You seem to believe in nothing.

Dr. C. That's my disease.

Edana. But surely—surely you believe in your work. (*He shakes his head and smiles.*) Then why have you taken so much trouble with all my poor people?

Dr. C. Mere force of habit. I've got into the way of curing people just as some folks get into the way of giving coppers to beggars. It relieves our feelings, but it's a very bad habit.

Edana. A bad habit to give life? A bad habit to relieve pain? Oh, I won't have you speak like this. I'm sure life is good. It's good to have it! It's good to give it! It is! It is! I don't under-stand you.

Dr. C. How is that?

Edana. You're so kind and gentle to everybody, and so sad and bitter against everything. I've often thought I'd ask you to tell me your history. You've had some great sorrow? (*She looks at him very sympathetically—he assents.*) Ah! (*She makes a sympathetic gesture towards him, looks at him with real sympathy.*) But you'll get over it—you'll conquer it.

DR. C.   I have conquered it.   But it has left me
hopeless.   My youth lies all behind me.   I'm alone
in the world.   I'm like a traveller who turns in to
rest at an inn for an hour or two—when I leave you
and go out to take up my journey again, I see thirty
years of life in front of me.   The shadow lies upon
all of them.

EDANA.   Oh, I'm so sorry for you!   No, I'm not!
You're young yet!   It's a shame—it's a shame to
despair! with all your gifts! and just in the prime of life.

DR. C.   Go on!   Go on!

EDANA.   Oh, if I could show you your future as I
see it!   Can't you see how splendid it might be?
You have the knowledge and the skill!   You are
loved and believed in!   You've only to put your hand
to it and to do it.

DR. C.   Go on!   Go on!

EDANA.   Oh, I wish I had your power!   I wish I
could make people well and glad!   I wish I could
give back a dying wife to her husband, or a dying
child to its mother.   Oh, I must make you do it.   Do
you hear?   You must go back to London and take
up your work!   You mustn't waste your time here!
You must go!

DR. C.   Don't send me away—at least, not yet.
Let me stay in my half-way house for a little while
longer, and then perhaps by and by I may feel stronger
to go on my journey.   Besides, you forget, I came to
Fontleas for a purpose.

EDANA.   To cure Mr. Amphiel—I can't think why he stays away so long.

DR. C.   You've not heard from him lately?

EDANA.   Not for the last fortnight.

DR. C.   And then he was at Genoa?

EDANA.   Yes, and wrote he should most likely take the first boat back.   I wish he had stayed at Fontleas to see you.

DR. C.   He left the very day before I came, didn't he?

EDANA.   Yes.   My father happened to say you were coming and that started him away.   I told you he dislikes to see doctors.

DR. C.   But he says the long voyage has restored him?

EDANA (*shakes her head*).   He says so.   He will never own to being ill.   But I fear—oh, my instinct tells me he is not better—that he never will be better.

DR. C.   Why do you fear that?

EDANA.   I don't know.   For the last two years he has been growing gradually worse—I'm sure of it—I can't shut my eyes to it.   If he should die!

DR. C.   You love him very much?

(*She looks at him.   He turns away and shows pain.*)

EDANA.   You will stay at Fontleas, won't you, till you've cured him?   I have such faith in you.

DR. C.   Have you?

EDANA.   I've watched you with my poor people. I don't know what it is—you are so different from most doctors. Tell me—there is something strange about you—something almost miraculous?

DR. C. (*shakes his head, smiles*). No. Nothing more miraculous than the everyday perpetual miracle of the power of the mind, will, soul, spirit—call it what you like—over the body. We none of us understand it. It's the very mystery of life itself. And when a case interests me I can't leave it. I feel ready to give part of my own life to my patient.

EDANA. Suppose Mr. Amphiel's case interested you?

DR. C. Then I would give up myself entirely to him if——

EDANA. If what?

DR. C. If in return you would heal me.

EDANA. What do you mean?

DR. C. I've gone astray. I've lost my clue. When I came here three months ago I had no faith, no hope, no wish to live. The night before I left town I had almost decided to end it.

EDANA. Ah, no

DR. C. Yes. It was the thought of you that kept me from it, the thought that I might be of some little use and help to you. Since I've been here with you I have gradually found my faith returning to me. I begin to believe again. Ah! it's true, this power that one soul has over another. Don't turn away from me! Heal me!

EDANA. Heal you! I heal you, the great London physician! What can I heal you of?

DR. C. My blindness! my darkness! You have the wisdom of life for me. You can give me back my youth, my faith. You can make me believe in myself, in my work—you can put together for me all the broken pieces of this puzzle of a world. Oh! it's wise to believe! It's wise to love! Heal me!

(*She goes and sits on the well.*)

EDANA. The country people say that if you look long enough into the well you can see Saint Edana's image in the waters.

DR. C. (*goes and looks down*). I can see her! She is in white! I believe in her powers. (EDANA *draws back.*) Give me one cup of water from her well.

(EDANA *looks at him, then goes and fills the stone cup and gives it to him.* DR. CAREY *takes the cup and drinks.*)

As he is drinking very reverently, LADY VALERIE, *very handsomely dressed, enters at the wicket gate* R. *and comes down.*

LADY V. How d'ye do?

DR. C. How d'ye do?   (*Bowing.*)

LADY V. I've interrupted a tête-à-tête. I'm so sorry. (*Glancing at* EDANA.) Perhaps your friend will forgive me.

DR. C. (*introducing*). Miss Hinde—Lady Valerie Camville.

LADY V. (*shaking hands with* EDANA). How do

you do? We've been terribly concerned in town about Dr. Carey. We lost him suddenly, and the wildest rumours have been afloat. So, as I was staying at Buxenham, I thought I'd drive over and learn the truth. (*To* Dr. Carey, *glancing at* Edana.) I've brought you a message from a friend of yours.

Edana. It's a little chilly, I'll step over to the Vicarage and get my shawl.   (*Exit* Edana, r.)

Lady V. (*looking after her*).   Lewin, I think she's charming.

Dr. C.   I scarcely expected to see you in Fontleas.

Lady V. Evidently not. Or I'm sure you wouldn't have been so ungallant as to choose the very moment of my arrival for making love to another woman.

Dr. C. You are mistaken. I was not making love to Miss Hinde.

Lady V. Oh, my dear Lewin, I heard you as I came along; no woman who has been really loved ever mistakes that accent. You forget that you have piped that same tune to me.

Dr. C.   No, not that tune.

Lady V. Yes, that same tune. It's always the same, like a bullfinch's ditty. There are only three notes in it—but oh, what music!

Dr. C. Miss Hinde is engaged to Mr. Walter Amphiel, and is devotedly attached to him.

Lady V. Is she? Then why pipe to her if she won't dance? Why waste your music on her when I should be rather glad to hear a note or two of the old tune?

DR. C.   What has brought you to Fontleas?

LADY V.   I've been bored.   I've had a horrible whiff of middle-age the last few weeks.

DR. C.   You!   Impossible!

LADY V.   I smell autumn—I scent it from afar. I ask myself how many years shall I have a man for my willing, devoted slave?   How many more years shall I be able by putting on my winningest airs and graces to extract some sort of homage from him? How many more years shall I have to mope, and wither, and remember, and attend church regularly? Oh, my God!   Lewin, it never can be worth while for a woman to live one moment after she has ceased to be loved.   (*He laughs a little, bitter, amused laugh; she breaks out rather fiercely.*)   And you men have the laugh of us!   Age doesn't wither you or stale your insolent, victorious, self-satisfied, smirking, common-place durability!   Oh, you brutes, I hate you all, because you're warranted to wash and wear for fifty years!   (*He laughs again.*)   Don't laugh at me!   I'm nearly mad!   Lewin, I've got another good ten years before me to be loved in, haven't I?   At least five. Tell me the truth—no, don't—give me what love you have to give while I'm attractive and worth it, and then—the moment I'm off colour—wht—a flash of lightning or an opium pill and have done with me!

DR. C.   And only three months ago you refused

the best love I had to offer.   Why did you do it?
You had met somebody else?

LADY V.   Don't ask me!   I was soon undeceived.
My dear Lewin, you don't know what a charming man
you are.   But I do, *now*.

DR. C.   Now!

LADY V.   And you're in love with that yard and
three-quarters of white muslin.   It won't last, you
know.

DR. C.   I'm not in love with her.   (LADY VALERIE
shakes her head.)   At least, I may not be.   I came here
jaded, disappointed, heartsick, heart-broken.   I met
her—a pure, bright girl, fresh from God's hands——

LADY V.   Fresh from *where?*

DR. C.   Oh, some of you do come from *there*, you
know!

LADY V.   Hum!   I shouldn't have thought it!
But you're a physician and you ought to know.
My dear Lewin, you don't really believe that stale
old legend.

DR. C.   What stale old legend?

LADY V.   The legend of Saint Edana: that a
woman can reform a man, change his character,
spiritualise him, etherealise him, pure-white-muslinise
him.

DR. C.   I've known an instance of it.

LADY V.   Your own.   But the process isn't com-
plete.   You've only known her three months, and she
has always worn white muslin.   You've known me six

years and I have never worn white muslin, or its accompanying inward and spiritual graces.

DR. C. They wouldn't suit you.

LADY V. Not now perhaps. But I had a white muslin period, when I came bright and pure and fresh from (*with an upward nod*) you know where—at least the boy who loved me thought I did. That was when I was seventeen.

DR. C. I can't see you in the character.

LADY V. Yet I have played it. Really, Lewin, in your profession you ought to have some knowledge of us and our trade secrets. Don't you know what women are?

DR. C. No. I've become a very simple greenhorn down here. Tell me, are you all alike?

LADY V. At heart, yes. We all go through the seven ages of women and play our trumpery little parts—all of them as artificial and tiresome as the French stage *ingénue*. In a few years Miss Hinde will be playing this *rôle*.

DR. C. She'll never be like you.

LADY V. No, but she'll be playing this part, and playing it—oh, not nearly so well as I do.

DR. C. She'll never be like you. You women don't even know your own sex.

LADY V. No? Perhaps not. But we get an occasional glimmer, whereas you men are quite in the dark. Oh, why won't you be content to know us and take us for what we are?

DR. C.   What are you?

LADY V.   Terrestrial-celestial amphibians.   Come!
You're to come back to Buxenham and dine with me.

DR. C.   I'm sorry.   I'm going to supper at the
Vicarage.

LADY V.   To-morrow, then?

DR. C.   I fear not.   I'm living in the quietest
way——

LADY V.   I know.   I've been down the lane to
see that queer old place where you live—the Abbot's
Kitchen, don't you call it?   Aren't you horribly dull?

DR. C.   I've been in worse company than my own.

LADY V.   Lewin, I'm sorry, terribly sorry that I
threw you over.   I want to hear a note or two of the
old tune.

DR. C.   It's too late.   (*Looking off.*)

LADY V.   I can't bear to lose you.   Sir Francis
Dumby's house is to let in Harley Street.   Come
back to London and let all be as it was, except that
I shall have learned to value you.

DR. C.   It's too late.   (*Looking off.*)

LADY V.   You can see some white muslin amongst
the trees.

DR. C.   Hush!   Her father.

Enter REV. PEREGRINE, R.

REV. P.   Ah, Doctor!

DR. C. (*presenting*).   Mr. Hinde—Lady Valerie
Camville.

LADY V. (*bows*). I must be getting back to Buxenham to dinner. Good-bye, Mr. Hinde. I should like to come and see over your church some day.

REV. P. Delighted, Lady Valerie. We prefer people who come to worship and to pray—or even to contribute to the offertory. Still we don't mind showing it to satisfy a reasonable curiosity. I'll show you over myself. Come any day.

LADY V. I will. I'm making a long stay in Buxenham.

DR. C. A long stay?

LADY V. Yes. My hearing is growing a little defective. I mean to stay at Buxenham to recover one or two lost notes, and you shall treat me. My carriage is at the inn—come and see me to it. Do you hear? Come and see me to my carriage!

> (*They go off at wicket gate* R., REV. PERE-
> GRINE *follows them up, humming, and
> looks after them.*)

Enter, R., JAMES HEBBINGS *and* LOUISA PACK, *a pair of country sweethearts.* JAMES *has his arm very tightly clasped round* LOUISA'S *waist with a defiant air of proprietorship.*

JAMES. Evenin', pa'son.

REV. P. Good evening, James. You seem very happy.

JAMES (*beaming, giggling. Tightly clasping her round the waist.* LOUISA *curtseys*). Me and Louisa have made up our minds to bring it off. That is as soon as we can save up a fi' pound note to give us a bit of a start.

REV. P. I'm glad to hear it, James.

LOUISA. Jim has been off and on for the last eighteen months, and I thought it was time for him to toe the mark.

JAMES. Well, Loo, I have toed the mark, like a man. Only in my judgment nobody ought to get married under a fi' pound note. In case of accidents, eh, pa'son?

REV. P. I commend your prudence, James. And, James, don't you think it would look prettier if you were to give your *arm* to Louisa?

JAMES (*blankly*). What for? I be going to be married to her, and if I bain't to put my arm round her waist, what be I to do?

REV. P. I wouldn't, James—in public.

JAMES (*takes his arm away very reluctantly*). I don't see as there's anything unreasonable about it. And it's allays been the way of courting in this parish.

REV. P. It is the way of courting in a great many parishes, still it is not a choice way of courting in any parish. Now, allow me. (*Disengaging* LOUISA *from* JAMES.) Observe, James,—this is how you were courting.

(*Putting his arm round* LOUISA *as* JAMES *had done.*)

LOUISA (*giggling*).   Don't 'ee, pa'son.

REV. P.   It is not an elegant attitude, James.

LOUISA.   Don't 'ee, pa'son.   (*Giggling.*)

REV. P.   It is only an object lesson, Louisa.   Now, James, when I go courting again—I'm sixty-seven (*sighs*)—this is the way I shall walk with my lady-love. Take my arm, Louisa.

LOUISA.   Oh, pa'son.

>   .   (REV. PEREGRINE HINDE *walks her up and down a few paces, then hands her over to* JAMES, *who has stood a little nonplussed and embarrassed.*)

REV. P.   There, James !   Take her.   Cherish her. Let her be as the loving hind and the pleasant roe, but don't fondle her indiscriminately in public.

JAMES (*giving* LOUISA *his arm*).   All same, pa'son, this way of courting 'ull never drive out the other way.
>   (*Taking* LOUISA *off at gate* L.)

REV. P.   It needn't, James—in private.
>   (*Exeunt* JAMES *and* LOUISA *at gate* L.)

Enter, R., JOHN DIBLEY *and* MARTHA DIBLEY, *a very aged, infirm old couple, supporting each other.*

REV. P.   Well, John, and how are you to-night, John ?

DIBLEY.   Oh, I be 'nation wellnigh blind, thank God ; and I ain't very clever in my insides, thank God ; and I 'spect I be about doubled up and done for, thank God; but otherways there ain't much the matter with me, thank God!

Rev. P. (*to* Mrs. Dibley). I'm glad to see you at church again, Martha.

Martha. Yes, pa'son. I feel somehow as I can't keep away from the old place.

Rev. P. That's right, Martha. It does you good?

Martha. Oh no, pa'son! We don't come to church for the good as we can get out of it.

Rev. P. Then why do you 'come to church, Martha?

Martha. You see, pa'son, when we've sot ourselves down comfortable for the sermon and you begin a-holding forth, I feel my old man's hand a-creeping towards mine, and mine a-creeping towards hisen, and I know he's a-thinking of our two boys as lay just outside the church a few foot off, eh, John?

John. Aye, aye!

Martha. And we sit there and we fancy as they're back again with us, and we're all one family again.

Rev. P. It's no fancy, Martha. We shall all be members of that family before long. And a very large family it will be.

John. Aye, aforelong, thank God! Come along, old woman! (*As they creep off towards the wicket gate* L.) Come along.

(*Exeunt* John *and* Martha Dibley *at wicket gate* L.)

Enter EDANA, R., *with* MARAH, *a child about five.*

MARAH. But where's my mammy? And where's my father?

EDANA. You have one Father—in Heaven——

MARAH. I've never seen Him! Why doesn't He come down here sometimes? I mean a real live father like other little girls have. There's your father. (*Pointing to* REV. PEREGRINE HINDE.) Where's mine?

(DR. CAREY *enters wicket gate* R.)

EDANA. I'll lend you my father sometimes. He's a very nice father, indeed. You couldn't have a better.

MARAH. But where's my mammy? I think I should like you for a mammy——

EDANA. Hush, dear. (*Kisses her, hides her face, looks up.*) What are you thinking of, Dr. Carey?

DR. C. The old mystery. The how and the why of love. The how and the why of life. (*She kisses the child again and hides her head behind her.*) It's very wonderful. And the more the microscope tells us about the how, the less we know about the why. What's your name, my pretty one? (*To* EDANA.) Who is she?

EDANA. Her name is Marah.

Enter, R., STEPHEN GURDON, *a man about sixty, a stern broken man, with strong features, and a settled hopeless look upon them.*

EDANA.   Here is her grandfather !
> (STEPHEN GURDON *sits on seat* R., *nodding to the* REV. PEREGRINE HINDE.)

REV. P.   Well, Stephen?

STEPHEN (*curtly*).   Pa'son.
> (*Sits, looks steadily in front of him.*)

DR. C. (*in a low tone to* REV. PEREGRINE).   What's the story?

REV. P.   He had an only daughter—she was betrayed, poor child—ran away from home and came back with that little one.   We tried to keep her here, and bring her back to the fold, but she ran away again and went utterly astray—sank and disappeared.   God have mercy on her and save her yet!   The mother broke her heart and died.   He broke his heart, but he lives on, poor man!

STEPHEN (*seeing they are whispering*).   Telling over my old tale again, pa'son?   You ain't got no call to do that.

REV. P.   But we can't help feeling sympathy with you.

STEPHEN.   Can't you?   Well, try and help it, pa'son.   I don't want your sympathy.

REV. P.   Very well, Stephen ; we'll keep it till you do.   Won't you soften your heart and come with us to-night, Stephen?

STEPHEN. No, I don't believe the stuff, and I won't say that I do. I'd as lief be left alone, pa'son.

REV. P. Very well, Stephen. But remember we keep open house here. (*Exit into church.*)

EDANA (*following* REV. PEREGRINE HINDE). Dr. Carey, aren't you coming to church?

DR. C. I promised to go and dress that poor fellow's leg. And I forgot all about him listening to you.

EDANA. You'll come back——?

DR. C. Yes. And if I don't come inside, look for me at the lepers' window.

(*Pointing to the lepers' window.*)

EDANA. No, you are healed now.

DR. C. Am I? You are my physician.

(*Exit wicket gate* R. EDANA *goes into church.*)

STEPHEN. Come here, Marah. Keep beside me.

MARAH (*goes to him*). Grandpa, what makes you so angry always? Can't you laugh?

STEPHEN. Oh yes, my chick. (*With a bitter, contemptuous laugh.*) I can laugh. (*Laughs again.*) I can laugh!

(*The child looks at him frightened.* AMPHIEL *appears at the wicket gate* R. ; *enters without seeing them, then catching sight of them is about to retreat, but* MARAH *sees him.*)

MARAH. Look, grandpa! Mr. Amphiel.

> (AMPHIEL *comes up to them. He looks some-
> what dissipated and haggard. His
> manner is furtive and constrained.*)

AMPHIEL. Stephen——

STEPHEN (*looks up and curtly nods*). Mr. Amphiel,
you're back home——

AMPHIEL. Yes, rather unexpectedly.

STEPHEN. You haven't happened to meet with
Jessie in any of your travels, I suppose?

AMPHIEL. No. I promised you I'd keep a good
look-out for her in all the towns where I go, and so I
will. But I've not been in England lately—I've been
to India.

STEPHEN. Ah!

AMPHIEL. But I shall be visiting a few of the
large towns on temperance work shortly, and I will
have some inquiries made. You may be sure I will
do everything I can to find her for you.

STEPHEN. You remember Jessie as a girl, don't
you?

AMPHIEL. Oh, very well—very well indeed.

STEPHEN. She was a handsome, strapping girl,
wasn't she? (*Turning to* MARAH.) Do you see the
likeness?

AMPHIEL. Hush! hush! (*To* MARAH.) Marah,
run away for a moment. I want to talk to your
grandfather. (*The child goes over,* R.) I wish I could
find your daughter. But I fear it's not likely.

STEPHEN. No, and if you did, what would she be like now? After six years of that! What's she doing to-night? Look! (*pointing to the sunset*) it's a beautiful evening, ain't it? And this is a hell of a world, ain't it?

AMPHIEL. Oh, don't speak like that. Mr. Gurdon, tell me, is there anything I can do to help you, to comfort you?

STEPHEN. Yes, bring me word that she's dead, so that I may know my own flesh and blood ain't hawking itself about from gin-shop to gin-shop this beautiful evening. (*Going off wicket gate* L.) Come along, Marah. I wonder what she's like to-night! I wonder what she's like to-night! (*Exit wicket gate* L.)

(MARAH *is crossing to follow him ;* AMPHIEL, *who has stood horrified, intercepts her as she passes him.*)

AMPHIEL. Marah, kiss me, my dear. (*Kisses her hungrily.*) Marah, when you grow up—you won't— you won't—kiss me, dear; promise me you'll grow up to be a good girl?

STEPHEN (*voice heard off*). Come, Marah!

MARAH. Hark! Grandpa!

AMPHIEL. But promise me——

MARAH. Yes, of course. I shall always be good. I promise you; there! (*Kisses him.*)

AMPHIEL. My dear, my dear!

(*Stroking her hair affectionately. She breaks away from him, runs off after* STEPHEN.

AMPHIEL *follows her a few steps. From this time stage gradually grows darker. Singing in the church.* AMPHIEL *goes to the lepers' window, looks in, shows great emotion, stretches out his hands with a vain, longing gesture. As the music swells he tumbles against the church wall, sobbing violently.*)

(*After a pause* EDANA *re-enters from the church behind him. She stands a moment or two watching him, then comes up to him, touches his shoulder.*)

EDANA. Walter! (*He turns round.*) Walter! I saw you through the window. You've come back? (*He turns round startled, rises, looks dazed, bewildered.*) Walter! What is it, dear? What ails you?

AMPHIEL. I don't know—the thought of the crowd in church—I'm always moved by the sight of a crowd. Don't take any notice of me. I'm better.

EDANA. I'm so glad you've come back! I've been so anxious about you. Where have you been? When did you land?

AMPHIEL. I've been in England some days. I didn't tell you because I wanted so much to start the new refuge at Plymouth. I felt it was my duty. I only finished very late last night—too late to telegraph you. So I came on at once.

EDANA. I might have known you had been at

some good work. But I've been so anxious! You should have written to me! Never mind! You're here! You're here! I can't tell you how glad I am! (*Crying a little with joy.*) Now it's I who am foolish! I'm so pleased to see you! Let me look at you! (*He turns away from her.*) No, let me look at you. I want to see if you are better.

AMPHIEL. I'm well enough. The voyage has done me a world of good. (*Avoiding her scrutiny.*)

EDANA (*very anxiously*). Are you sure? Oh, my dearest, you look ill—you look very ill.

AMPHIEL. No, no. Only a little tired. That's all.

EDANA. Dr. Carey shall see you in the morning.

AMPHIEL. Dr. Carey? Is he still here? Why hasn't he gone back?

EDANA. He has given up his practice and is living here. I've talked to him so much about you. He has promised to take you thoroughly in hand and look after you till you're quite well.

AMPHIEL. I tell you there's nothing the matter with me. I'm quite well! I won't see him!

EDANA. Yes, yes, dearest—to please me. Say it's only my whim, but do, do see him. Oh, my dearest, you don't know how I care for you. My heart is like stone when I think of you.

AMPHIEL. I'm not worth it. Don't trouble about me. I'm not worth it.

EDANA. Oh yes, indeed you are, and I must have

you well.   Oh, I've so much to tell you.   But tell me about yourself first.

AMPHIEL.   Edana, since I've been in India I've formed a great plan.

EDANA.   Yes, dear, tell me.

AMPHIEL.   It depends on you whether I carry it out or not.

EDANA.   If it depends on me you know it is done —if it is anything within my power.　　ˎ

AMPHIEL.   Dare you give up everything for the cause, and for me?

EDANA.   Try me and see.

AMPHIEL.   You know, dear, that at times I have a dreadful nausea of life and feel obliged to hide away from my fellow-creatures for a while, and then nothing brings me round but a plunge into my work.

EDANA.   Ah, dear, you work too hard.

AMPHIEL.   No, no, it's my work that keeps me alive.   Edana, I feel that if I were to leave England altogether——

EDANA.   For life?

AMPHIEL.   For some years.   There's a tremendous field for temperance work in India.   There, the fiend is opium.   Here, it's alcohol.   But the craving, the disease, is the same.

EDANA.   And you would go to India to live?

AMPHIEL.   Dare I ask it of you?

EDANA.   My father!

AMPHIEL.   Ah! I knew it was too much to ask.

EDANA. No, no! I'll do it if it is the best for
you. I gave myself to you and I won't draw back.
Yes, Walter, when you ask me I shall be ready.

AMPHIEL. Oh, I'm not worthy of you!

EDANA. Not worthy of me? Oh, you are far
better and braver than I am. I love you for your
devotion to your work! There's not another man in
the world like you.

> (DR. CAREY *has entered wicket gate* R., *and has*
> *come upon them to overhear the last words,*
> *and to see her looking up to* AMPHIEL
> *with the greatest devotion. He sees*
> AMPHIEL—*a momentary glance of recog-*
> *nition between the two men.* AMPHIEL
> *shows fright and mutely appeals to* DR.
> CAREY. DR. CAREY *shows great moment-*
> *ary surprise with horror, which he*
> *quickly conceals.*)

DR. C. I beg pardon——   (*Is going.*)

EDANA. No, Dr. Carey, don't go. I want to
introduce you. Mr. Amphiel—Dr. Carey.

> (AMPHIEL *again makes mute appeal to* DR.
> CAREY.)

AMPHIEL. How d'ye do, Dr. Carey?

> (*Offers hand, which* CAREY *takes after slight*
> *reluctance.*)

DR. C. How d'ye do?

EDANA (*to* DR. CAREY). There is your patient.
He has come at last. (*To* AMPHIEL.) You are to

put yourself entirely in his hands and do exactly as he tells you, and (*very excitedly*) you will, you will for my sake?

> (AMPHIEL *looks at* DR. CAREY *with mingled apprehension and appeal.*)

DR. C. (*significantly looking at* AMPHIEL). I'm sure Mr. Amphiel will trust himself to me, and I shall give him every care and attention.

EDANA (*to* AMPHIEL). There! Now I'm satisfied! I feel you are well already.

> (MARAH *runs in at wicket gate* L., *and comes up to* EDANA.)

EDANA. I feel so happy! I haven't got over the thought that you are here! Ah, Marah!

> (*Seizes the child, kisses her.* AMPHIEL *makes a movement to stop her, which* EDANA *does not notice; it is, however, seen by* DR. CAREY, *who for the moment does not understand it; turns round to notice* STEPHEN, *who enters wicket gate* L. DR. CAREY'S *face shows a sudden illumination of horror; he turns to* AMPHIEL, *who appeals to him.* DR. CAREY *stands horror-stricken.*)

EDANA (*hugging* MARAH). Oh, I'm so happy, Marah, so happy! You must come with me and I must give you something to make *you* happy. (*To* AMPHIEL.) You're to tell him everything and then come on to the Vicarage to me. I've so much to talk

about! Come, Marah. (*To* STEPHEN.) I'm going
to take her with me, Mr. Gurdon. Come and fetch
her by and by. (*To* AMPHIEL.) Don't be long! I'm
waiting for you! Don't be long!

   (*Exit,* R., *fondling* MARAH. STEPHEN *follows.*
    DR. CAREY, *as soon as* EDANA *and*
    MARAH *have gone off, allows himself*
    the full expression of his horror to
    AMPHIEL, *points to* STEPHEN'S *retreating*
    figure. AMPHIEL *stands abject, appeal-*
    ing. Exit STEPHEN, R.)

AMPHIEL (*in a whisper*). You won't betray me?

·DR. C. My God! My God! You! You to be
her husband?

AMPHIEL. You won't betray me? (*Agonized.*)
You won't betray me?

DR. C. Betray you? No! But you'll break off
this engagement.

AMPHIEL. I can't! I can't! I love her so much.
And she loves me. It would break her heart. I can't
give her up! I'll make myself worthy of her. It's
not too late! I can do anything for her sake. I can
conquer myself and I will! Help me! You're a
physician. She said you could cure me. Will you?
Will you? I throw myself on your mercy! Save me!

DR. C. (*hesitates for a few moments. He looks very*
searchingly at AMPHIEL, *seizes* AMPHIEL'S *hands, makes*
AMPHIEL *look at him. Hymn in church*). Will you
put yourself in my hands from this moment? Will

you give yourself over to me, do as I bid you, be guided by me in everything, till I have done my best to heal you, made a new man of you, so far as that is possible? Will you do it?

AMPHIEL. Yes, yes—anything. And you'll save me from myself?

DR. C. Trust to me! Whatever human skill and patience can do, I'll do for you, and I'll never leave you while there's a hope that I can drag you out of this mire and make you fit to hold up your head before all men, and before her! Trust to me, my poor lad, trust to me!

CURTAIN.

(*Six months pass between Acts II. and III.*)

GROUND PLAN OF ACT III.

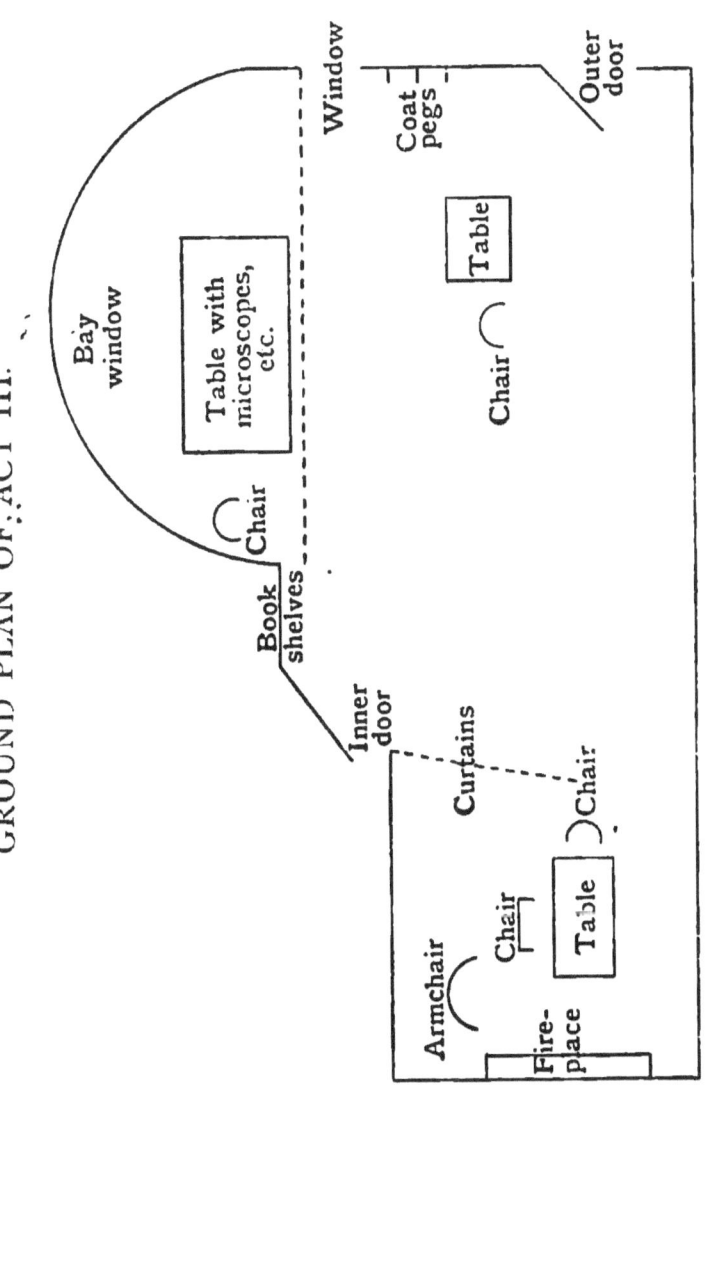

ACT III

Scene—The Abbot's Kitchen at Fontleas, a very
    quaint, irregular Gothic Building adapted
    to a modern living-room, with Evidences of
    frequent Restoration and Alteration.

On the R. *down stage a large old-fashioned fireplace with
ornaments and photographs, one of them a photograph
of* Amphiel *and* Edana *taken together. Above the
fireplace a large old-fashioned armchair, very deep ; a
small table on castors is laid with the remains of
dinner for two. Chairs above and to* L. *of table.
The whole of this* R. *side of the room is curtained in
and forms a cosy nook—the curtains of heavy dark
material run from an angle in the wall up stage to
within about two yards of the footlights, and are
hung on a brass rod suspended from the ceiling,
which is rather low. Above and in line with the
curtains is a door, called throughout the Act the
inner door. All the* L. *side of the stage at back is
taken up with a deep recess and bay window. In
this recess is a large table with microscopes, glass*

bottles, *tubes, scientific instruments and apparatus, books, papers, MSS., scientific periodicals, etc. At the sides of the recess and under the bay window are shelves filled with scientific books, and there are heaps of books on the floor in the recess. The window looks out upon a wintry night landscape with moon. The window and recess are also curtained off by curtains. These curtains run 'across* R. *and* L. *The space to the* L. *makes a kind of hall, and is carpeted but sparely furnished, one or two chairs and a small table somewhat to the* L. *In the* L. *wall a window up stage, and a very large thick old oak door with heavy handle and lock and key down stage. Between the window and door on the* L. *are several pegs with hats, overcoats, and an umbrella stand with umbrella and sticks.*

TIME : *about half-past seven on a December evening.*

Discover DR. CAREY *and* BROOKER *at the little table* R., *curtained in by the curtain running down stage from the inner door.* DR. CAREY *is on the chair above the table,* BROOKER *on a chair at the side of the table. The curtains running across the stage are also drawn, shutting off the table and scientific apparatus. They have just finished dinner, and a bright fire is burning.*

DR. C.   Well, I told you I was equal to a plain dinner.

BROOKER. Excellent. A cutlet, a cold chicken, and a bottle of seventy-five claret, what can a man want more?

DR. C. And you really took me by surprise.

BROOKER. I had the afternoon to spare. I looked up "Bradshaw," found I could just catch a train, have an hour with you, and get back by the late express. What a confounded queer place to live in, Carey!

(*Looking round the place.*)

DR. C. Yes, it was the kitchen belonging to the old abbey. It tumbled into decay and got turned into a farmhouse. It tumbled into decay again, the farmer himself tumbled into decay, and died; his widow sold off the land, patched the old place up, and made it just fit for me to live in.

BROOKER. And you can really live here all alone?

DR. C. Not all alone. I have two human companions, and some millions of microbes.

BROOKER. And where are they, the human companions?

DR. C. My housekeeper, old Granny Barton, is racked with rheumatism, so I've sent her over to Buxenham for a course of treatment, and her neighbour Mrs. Bowden comes in and does for me. Then I've one patient, Mr. Walter Amphiel—fill your glass.

BROOKER (*filling glass*). Amphiel, the Temperance organiser—does he let you drink seventy-five claret?

DR. C. No. I've not tasted wine for the last six

months, all the time he has been with me.   But he's
away just now.

BROOKER.   Oh—where is he?

(MRS. BOWDEN, *a stout, pleasant-looking
country woman in bonnet and shawl,
enters at inner door, draws aside the
curtains.*)

DR. C.   Well, Mrs. Bowden, going for the night?

MRS. B.   Yes, doctor, unless there's anything I
can do for you.

DR. C.   Nothing, thank you.

MRS. B.   I suppose Mr. Amphiel won't be coming
back to-night?

DR. C. (*after a slight pause*).   No, I think not.

MRS. B.   I've left his room ready for him in case
he does.   And perhaps you'll excuse my going.   I've
got my man to look after, and he does rave and storm
the house down if his supper ain't ready to the minute.

DR. C.   Ah! husbands are tiresome animals, Mrs.
Bowden.

MRS. B. (*cordially*).   Oh they are, sir!   You know
'em, being a doctor.   Whatever possesses a gal to get
married when she's well off, I cannot think.   But the
chaps will come teasing and plaguing round us, and
we fools like it—and then, there it is—work and
worry and babies, work and worry and babies, nothing
else from the time you're twenty till you're wore out.
Oh dear, oh dear!   I do hope there's some good
purpose running through it all.

DR. C. I hope so, Mrs. Bowden. But the ways of Providence are dark.

MRS. B. Oh, they are, sir. You may well say that. Breakfast as usual, sir?

DR. C. Breakfast as usual, Mrs. Bowden.

MRS. B. Then I'll say good-night, sir. (*To* BROOKER.) And good-night to *you*, sir.

DR. C. Good-night, Mrs. Bowden!)
BROOKER. Good-night!   ` } (*Together.*)

> (*Exit* MRS. BOWDEN *at inner door. As she goes off,* DR. CAREY *rises, pushes chair back from table, further draws back the curtain.* BROOKER *moves his chair.* CAREY *pushes table a little out into centre of room and up towards the inner door—it remains there just on the right side of the curtain line during the remainder of Act.*)

DR. C. (*taking out watch*). You've half an hour yet, old fellow. Light your cigar and let's make the most of it.

BROOKER. How can you bury yourself in this hole, Carey?

DR. C. Hole? Bury myself? I've been living, Brooker, the last few months, really living for the first time in my life.

BROOKER. But you're wasting yourself down here.

DR. C. Wasting myself! I work from morning to night. (*Goes up to curtains, draws them aside, dis-*

*covers the back of the room and table with scientific
apparatus, etc.*)   Look!   (*Takes up a tube, holds it to*
BROOKER.)   Don't whisper it, Brooker, I fancy I'm
on the track of the cancer microbe!   I'm not sure I
haven't got my gentleman here.   And I shall have a
little to say and a great deal to do when the next
cholera outbreak comes.   You know I was always
more of a student than a practitioner.   I never had
quite a good bedside manner, Brooker.

BROOKER.   And you've quite made up your mind
not to come back to London?

DR. C.   Quite.   So settle yourself in Cavendish
Square, physic away, and say no more about it.

(*Goes rather restlessly to outer door, opens it,
looks out, shuts it.*)

BROOKER.   Are you expecting anybody?

DR. C.   No.   Only the evening post.

BROOKER.   Carey, I shan't like leaving you to-night.

DR. C.   Why not?

BROOKER.   There's something wrong with you.
I've been watching you.   You're feverish, restless,
unsettled.

DR. C.   Am I?

BROOKER.   What ails you?   Can an old friend
be of any help or comfort?

DR. C.   I'll tell you, Brooker.   I don't think I
could speak of this to anybody but you.   It's too
sacred.

BROOKER.   Go on!

DR. C.   I suppose most of us have been attracted and have lightly loved many women.   Those loves are not *love*.   And I suppose most of us have had, once in our lives, an overpowering passion.

BROOKER.   Yes.   Thank God, I got mine over early, when I was twenty-five.

DR. C.   And since then?

BROOKER.   Since then I've been too busy scraping together bread and cheese for Mrs. Brooker and my family to get into much mischief of that sort.   And now I hope I'm comfortably past the danger of making myself a fool for a woman.

DR. C. (*looking at him*).   You're not to be envied, Brooker.

BROOKER.   Perhaps not.   But Mrs. Brooker is. Go on.

DR. C.   You remember my coming down here last spring?   I was quite hopeless, except for the one thought that perhaps I might make Miss Hinde happy by restoring her lover to health.

BROOKER.   Well?

DR. C.   He went on a voyage to India.   Meantime I saw a great deal of her, helped her in her parish work, and doctored her invalids.   Brooker, before Amphiel came back, I couldn't disguise from myself that my whole future, my whole being, my whole life, were bound up in that girl.

BROOKER.   Nonsense, Carey!   Nonsense!   Nonsense!

DR. C. No, Brooker, Wisdom! Wisdom! From the moment I saw her, I became young and hopeful again. She has sweetened and blessed and renewed the whole earth for me. I tell you, Brooker, of all the millions around us she and I are the only living creatures on this earth.

BROOKER. Nonsense! Nonsense! Nonsense!

DR. C. No, Wisdom! Wisdom! Wisdom! If I had to part from her, I feel that moment I should drop back again into madness and despair. With her—with her—O my God! Brooker—with her what a splendid life I could live in this dull world for the next thirty years.

BROOKER. But you say she is engaged to Amphiel?

DR. C. Yes.

BROOKER. And she's attached to him?

DR. C. Devotedly attached.

BROOKER. And she doesn't suspect your feelings for her?

DR. C. She must know that I have a great regard for her, perhaps guesses that I love her. But so far as I have been able, I have been perfectly loyal to her, and to him.

BROOKER. Carey, this is madness, you know. It can't continue. Why don't you get away from this place and leave her to marry the fellow?

DR. C. I told you he is my patient.

BROOKER. Oh yes, of course. You said he'd

been living with you here for some months. (*Gets up to light his cigar, goes to fireplace.*)   Curious arrangement.   What's the matter with him ?   (*At that moment his eyes fall upon the photograph of* AMPHIEL *and* EDANA *which is on the shelf of the fireplace ; he shows some astonishment and takes up the photograph.*) Carey, whose portraits are these ?

DR. C.   That is Amphiel—and Miss Hinde, taken together.

BROOKER (*startled*).   This man Amphiel—this— Amphiel ?

DR. C.   Yes—why ?

BROOKER.   The young fellow who consulted you——

DR. C.   Of course.   You saw him that evening. I had forgotten.

BROOKER.   You forgot, too, that he had consulted me about four years before.   Carey, I wasn't mistaken —that man is a drunkard.

DR. C.   Yes.

BROOKER.   A hopeless drunkard ?

DR. C.   No—not quite hopeless, since he has been here with me.

BROOKER.   And she doesn't know ?

DR. C.   She hasn't the least thought of it.   She could see he was ill, and asked me to take him under my care.   I've had him hanging round my neck like a millstone for the last six months.

BROOKER.   Where is he now ?

Dr. C. I don't know. But I shall know in a few minutes—as soon as the post comes in.

(*Looking anxiously at the outer door.*)

Brooker. I don't understand—you seem——

Dr. C. I seem—what?

Brooker. You seem to be waiting for some bad news of him.

, Dr. C. I am! I hate him, Brooker! I may as well show you all my heart now I've begun. I hate him! Damn him! I hate him! for he stands between her and me. I brought him here to live with me; I've been alone with him all this while. I've scarcely let him go out of my sight. The strain has been awful. At times it has almost driven me mad. To sit here and talk to him, soothe him, amuse him, knowing all the while that the devil inside him was urging him to get away and ruin himself. I've been doctor, nurse, father, brother, friend to him. I never had such a task. But I've done it, because she loves him. And partly because the man interests me, fascinates me. Here's the strange thing—I hate him, but I want to save him. I began to feel proud of the case. I saw him growing brighter, happier, stronger every day. And it made her so happy. She was so grateful to me. Well, all went well with him till three weeks ago——

Brooker. What then?

Dr. C. He went out for a walk with her and persuaded her that his temperance work called him away. She believed him and came back alone. We got no news of him. She grew more and more anxious, and a week ago I went up to London and put the matter in the hands of Nicholson the private detective. I got this telegram from him this morning——

> (*Taking telegram from pocket and giving it*
> *to* BROOKER.)

BROOKER (*reading the telegram*). "Have discovered the person. Am writing you fully by this post. Nicholson." (*Giving back telegram to* DR. CAREY.) And you fear——

DR. C. Fear? No, Brooker—that's it—I don't fear—I almost hope. (*A postman's knock at outer door.*) The post ! (*Goes to door, opens it.*)

POSTMAN (*without, handing in letter*). Bitter cold again to-night, sir.

DR. C. (*taking letter*). Very cold.

POSTMAN. Good-night, sir.

DR. C. Good-night, Carter.

> (*Closes door, looking intently at letter.*)

BROOKER. From Nicholson?

DR. C. Yes. (*Opens letter watched by* BROOKER. *As he reads his face shows an intense stealthy interest, growing more and more eager, almost malignant. Very quiet hoarse tone denoting the utmost suppressed excitement.*) He has broken out, Brooker. They've found him in one of the lowest dens in Bristol. He has been there for some days. Last night he got away

from there — they don't know where. Read.
(BROOKER *takes letter*.) Oh, what a wretch I am to
rejoice that a man is ruined!

BROOKER (*reads*). "He was, however, in a much
calmer state last night, and had almost recovered.
He seems to have had some suspicion that he was
being watched, for during the evening he managed
to get away. We are making urgent inquiries for him
in every direction, and will let you know as soon as
we have traced him. We have carefully observed
your instructions concerning secrecy, and have not
allowed his name to transpire." Got away? What
do you suppose has become of him?

DR. C. How should I know? Am I his keeper?
Haven't I done my best? For the last six months
I've held that man from slipping over the precipice.
If I had let go my hold for one moment he would
have dropped. Now he has tumbled in spite of me!
Well, I can't help it. I've done with him! I give
him up! Am I not justified? Eh? Eh? Am I
not justified?

BROOKER. Carey! Carey!

DR. C. You know I'm justified! I am! I am!
I gave him every chance, more than every chance.
I've fought for him against himself! I've kept suspicion away from her! I've watched him making love
to her day after day, and I've watched her lifting her
face to his with a look of that I'd whistle my soul
away to get from her. Now that's all past! It's

going to be my turn! I'm free of him and she shall
be free of him.   Yes, I understand her nature, she
won't love him when she knows the truth.

BROOKER.   And you'll let her know?

DR. C.   How can I help it?   Why should I try
to hinder it?

> (*A knock at the outer door.   During the above
> speeches* BROOKER *has unobtrusively laid
> the letter on the table* R.)

DR. C.   Is it Amphiel?   (*Goes to door, opens it.*)

Enter EDANA *in outdoor winter dress.*

DR. C.   Miss Hinde.

EDANA.   You have a visitor.

DR. C. (*presenting*).   Doctor Brooker—Miss Hinde.

> (EDANA *bows.*)

BROOKER (*bowing*).   How d'ye do?   (*Takes out
watch.*)   Carey, I must be going.   (*Goes to* L. *side of
the room where his hat and overcoat are hanging, takes
them down.*)   I'm sorry to be leaving you, but I've
only just time to catch my train.

> (DR. CAREY *goes and helps him on with over-
> coat.   EDANA goes towards fire.*)

BROOKER.   How long will it take me to get to the
station?

DR. C.   About ten minutes.

BROOKER.   You'll let me know how this turns
out?

DR. C. Yes.

BROOKER. Good-night, Miss Hinde.

EDANA. Good-night, DR. Brooker.

BROOKER (*to* DR. CAREY). Good-bye.

DR. C. Good-bye. You're sure you know your way?

BROOKER. Oh yes. Carey, old fellow (*glancing at* EDANA), are you sure you know yours?

(A significant look.)

DR. C. I'll try and find it.

(Exit BROOKER *at outer door.)*

DR. C. (*closes door after* BROOKER *and comes to* EDANA, *very tenderly*). Miss Hinde.

EDANA. Have you heard anything of Walter?

DR. C. (*hesitates*). I hope I shall have some news for you in a day or two.

EDANA. In a day or two! But I can't wait. I feel sure he's in some danger or trouble. And I can't get to him!

DR. C. (*very searchingly, but without showing it to her*). Suppose you had to hear some bad news of him—you would be brave and bear it?

EDANA. What do you mean?

DR. C. You still wish to share in this great enterprise of his—you are still as much attached to his cause—and to him?

EDANA. Is there any need to ask me that? You know I am! Why do you ask me? You've heard something! He's dead!

DR. C. No. You needn't fear that.

EDANA. He's ill. You've had news. (*At this moment* DR. CAREY'S *eyes fall on the letter* BROOKER *has laid on the table* L. *She follows his glance.* DR. CAREY *takes up the letter.*) That letter! It's about him! Why don't you speak? Oh, why do you torture me?

DR. C. (*holding letter*). Miss Hinde, tell me, you know I wouldn't willingly torture you——

EDANA. I'm sure you wouldn't. But if that letter has news of Mr. Amphiel, let me see it—or at least tell me what it contains. (*Holding out her hand.*)

DR. C. (*his face shows a momentary struggle*). Tell me, you know that I would always do what I thought to be best for you and him—at least, best for you.

EDANA. I'm sure you would, but—I must know where he is. Why won't you tell me?

DR. C. I don't know, and this letter doesn't say. To read it would only add to your anxiety. Trust me. You've trusted me for many months past. Say that you'll trust me a little longer?

EDANA (*looks at him*). Yes, I will trust you.

DR. C. (*puts letter in pocket*). And rest assured we shall have some news of him before long.

EDANA. Ah, but when? Oh, I can't wait! I've not slept for three nights.

DR. C. Not slept for three nights!

(*A knock at outer door.* DR. CAREY *goes to it, opens it.*)

DR. C. Lady Valerie!

LADY VALERIE, *in very handsome widow's mourning, enters, followed by* SAUNDERS, *her maid, also in mourning.*

LADY V.   It's an unconscionable hour to call. But I see you do receive visitors as late as this. (*Glancing at* EDANA. *Bows to her.* EDANA *bows.*) Are you at home ?

DR. C.   Yes, certainly.   As soon as I've seen Miss Hinde safely to the Vicarage.

EDANA.   Oh, please no.

LADY V.   My maid shall go with you.

EDANA.   It's only a few steps across the fields, and there is a moon.   I won't have any one come with me.   Good-night, Lady Valerie.

LADY V.   Good-night.

EDANA.   Good-night, Dr. Carey.

DR. C.   Good-night.   Sleep well to-night.   You can and you will.

EDANA.   Oh, I can't.

DR. C.   Try.   Try.   And to-morrow we may have news !

EDANA.   Oh, I can't endure the suspense !

> (*Exit* EDANA *at outer door.* DR. CAREY *looks after her.*)

LADY V.   Saunders, you've had nothing since lunch.   Go to the inn and get something to eat. And wait for me there.

SAUNDERS.   Yes, my lady.

(DR. CAREY *holds the door open for* SAUNDERS *and closes it after her.*)

DR. C.   This is an unexpected pleasure——

LADY V.   Pleasure?

DR. C.   What brings you back here?

LADY V.   Boredom! Boredom! Boredom! Boredom devours me everywhere. Even burying one's husband has a smack of it. And widowhood, which in the distance seems a rosy paradise, is nothing but a Sahara when you get there. You don't seem very pleased to see me. Am I welcome?

DR. C.   I'll try to make you so.

LADY V.   You'll try? You're terribly frank.

DR. C.   Won't it be better for us to be quite honest with each other?

LADY V.   You talk as if we had tried the other policy and it hadn't quite succeeded.

DR. C.   I've always been quite honest with you— at least, in all the great things of life.

LADY V.   There are no great things in life, my poor Lewin. It's all very small beer, and very scanty skittles. (*Looking at the table.*) White muslin has been dining with you tête-à-tête?

DR. C.   No, my old friend Brooker. He has just left for London.

LADY V.   But white muslin was here. I'm horribly jealous—but I'm horribly hungry too.

DR. C.   And I've only cold chicken to offer you. But you are heartily welcome.

LADY V.   I am heartily welcome to your cold chicken.   Thank you.   I'll try your cold chicken.
(*Sitting down to table.*)

DR. C.   My servant has gone for the night, so I'm all alone.

(*A knock at outer door.   DR. CAREY goes to open it, opens it, telegraph boy hands in a telegram.   DR. CAREY closes door.*)

DR. C.   Allow me.

(*Opens telegram, reads it, shows great interest.*)

LADY V.   You're all alone.   Where is your patient Mr. Amphiel?

"DR. C.   He has been away.   Curiously enough, this telegram is from him.   He is coming back to-night.

(*A pause.   DR. CAREY stands much absorbed looking at the telegram.*)

LADY V.   What's the matter?   Has anything happened to him?

DR. C. (*recalling himself*).   No.   Nothing.

(*Puts telegram in pocket.*)

LADY V.   Then light your cigar and talk to me. But don't look at me while I'm eating.

DR. C.   Not look at you?

LADY V.   I'm sure your later theory is right. Women are entirely spiritual.   I constantly feel little shootings and sproutings about my shoulder-blades where my wings will be, and then isn't it disgusting? two or three times every day my hatefully healthy appetite drives me to toy with such gross realities as this. (*Holding up a chicken bone.*)   Oh, don't laugh at me!   If you knew how sad my heart is—(*deep sigh*) you never sent me a word, Lewin.

DR. C.   What could I say?

LADY V.   Any cut-and-dried message of condolence would have done.   It would have cost you nothing and it would have meant so much to me.   I wonder if any man ever guesses the exquisite agony a woman feels who waits and waits and waits for one word of love from the man to whom she has been all the world —and waits in vain.

DR. C.   I wonder if any woman ever guesses the exquisite agony a man feels who is thrown over by the woman who is all the world to him—thrown over for, perhaps, the first chance acquaintance.

LADY V.   No.   No.   There you're wrong.   It wasn't the first chance acquaintance.   Let it pass. You're mean to remind me of that,—as mean as a woman.

DR. C.   As mean as a woman!

LADY V.   Yes, that's the perpetual paradox of womanhood.   We are angels—I feel sure of it—and yet we do such mean things.   How do you account for it?

DR. C.   I can't.   I trust, meantime, you're making a comfortable dinner.

LADY V.   I feel as if I were picnicking on my mother's grave in the damp.

DR. C.   Why?

LADY V.   Cold chicken is as cold as cold shoulder.
But cold chicken and love make a divine hot collation.

DR. C.   I fear I have only cold chicken to offer
you.

LADY V.   (*shrugs her shoulders—goes on eating.
After a little pause*).   You haven't asked me about the
last' two months.

DR. C.   Tell me.

LADY V.   You know I got a telegram saying that
it was only a question of a few weeks.   So I went out
to.him at once.   I didn't wish to outrage the decent
hypocrisies whereby men live——

DR. C.   Men don't live by hypocrisies.

LADY V.   Well, society does.   And I've always
loyally respected them and lived up to them.   Well,
I went out to him and was perfectly kind and attentive
to him to the last.   And so ended the tragic farce of
my married life.   It's over.   I spent one month in
unselfishly nursing him—I spent the next month in
unselfishly devising a scheme of widow's mourning
that should spare my bereaved sisters the additional
pang of feeling themselves perfect frights during the
period of their greatest sorrow.   (*Gets up and comes
away from table.*)   How do you think I have succeeded?

> (*She has a long handsome cloak with black
> fur.   She stands with arms extended
> and with a little entreating gesture
> towards him.*)

Dr. C. (*coldly*). Admirably, I should say. But I'm no judge.

Lady V. Do you know what I was thinking all the time I was planning this mourning? I was thinking—will it give me one of my old moments of charm in his eyes? Or, if not, will it give me some new little grace or attraction?

> (*He does not reply. She stands for a moment with a little appealing gesture, then suddenly bursts into a tempest of tears.*)

Dr. C. Lady Valerie! (*She is sobbing.*) Lady Valerie, will you listen to me?

Lady V. No! No! No! Oh, I hate myself, and I hate you! I hate you! Oh! Oh! Oh! Let me go!

> (*He is between her and the door.*)

Dr. C. No. Hear me. I cannot give you the love I once offered you, and I have too tender a regard for the past and for you to offer you the ghost of it. Would you have me do it? Would you have me offer you a fiction, a lie? Would you have me pretend to love you, knowing that my whole heart, my every thought and hope and desire belong to another woman?

Lady V. But you can never marry her! (*A curious look of hope on* Dr. Carey's *face which she sees and interprets.*) She has broken off her engagement to Mr. Amphiel? Something has happened to him?

Dr. C. No. He is now on his way here.

LADY V.   Then what makes you so hopeful? You can never marry her.

DR. C.   No, perhaps not.

LADY V.   And you might come back to me.—It's not too late? it's not too late? you might change?
                                        (*Very imploringly.*)

DR. C.   I shall never change.   (*Very firmly.*)   I shall never change.

> (*She stands very hopeless for some seconds, then makes a shrug of resignation. Her manner changes, and is careless and off-hand till the end of the scene.*)

LADY V.   Very well. Put on your hat and coat and see me across to the inn. Put on your hat and coat. (*He takes his hat and coat.*) I want your advice.

DR. C.   Advice? About what?

LADY V.   Marriage. I can have Bertie Fewins or Sir George Doudney. Which shall it be?

DR. C.   Neither.

LADY V.   Oh, it must be one or the other. And it must be settled at once; so I shall get back by the mail to-night. (*Going towards outer door.*) Come.

DR. C.   This will be our nearest way to the George. It will save us the lane. Take my arm through the passage.   (*Indicating inner door.*)

LADY V. (*taking his arm*).   Which shall it be? Bertie or Sir George?

DR. C.   Neither! Neither! Why should it be either?

LADY V. My dear Lewin, what shall I be in five years' time if I don't marry somebody? What shall I do? I'm neither a saint nor a fool, so I can't stand perpetual church-going. No! It must be marriage. Bertie or Sir George?

DR. C. That won't be marriage, that will be desecration of a woman's soul!

LADY V. (*shakes her head, makes a face as if taking physic*). It's a devil of a world for women, Lewin. For God's sake don't moralise about it.

>(*Exeunt at inner door. A very long pause. A knock at outer door. The knock is repeated. The* REV. PEREGRINE HINDE *puts in his head at outer door and locks round.*)

REV. P. (*calling out*). Dr. Carey! Mrs. Bowden! Dr. Carey! (*Coming in.*) I came to Taffy's house. Taffy wasn't at home. (*Speaking off.*) There's nobody here.

Re-enter EDANA *at outer door.*

EDANA. Won't Dr. Carey think it strange of me coming again?

REV. P. No, no. I've got a waggon-load of excuses. He can't have gone far. We'll wait till he comes back. (*They go towards fire.*) There! Sit down! (*She sits in armchair.*)

EDANA. I'm sure he has had some news, and I'm

sure it's bad news. Oh, I must know—do you think
he'll tell us the truth?

REV. P. If he doesn't tell us, I must gently
wheedle it out of him. Have you ever studied the
composition of my character, Edana?

EDANA. No.

REV. P. No? Then you've never observed how
exquisitely Providence has blended in me the beautiful
transparent innocence of the dove with the subtle and
useful wisdom of the serpent. We'll begin by asking
him for some little sleeping draught——

EDANA. Oh, I cannot endure another night!

REV. P. Indeed you can. The human spirit can
endure unendurable things. There is nothing the
human spirit *cannot* endure. Come, come! (*Chafing
her hands.*) How cold these poor little paws are!
Put your head on the cushion! There! (*Arranging
her comfortably in armchair.*) Rest a little till Dr.
Carey comes. Now what shall I do to while away the
time? Shall I preach you a little sermon? Or shall
I tell you a little tale? Or shall I sing you a little
song? Or shall I do all three?

EDANA. All three. You don't think Walter is ill
—or dead? Oh, what shall I do?

REV. P. Hush! Hush! Hush! (*Soothes her
down.*) The times are not in our hands. (*From this
time she shows signs of drowsiness, until the middle of
the song, when she is fast asleep.*) Now, first the little
sermon. You should never put all your eggs in one

basket, unless that basket is made of celestial wicker-work and is safely stored away in heaven. That's the sermon. Its metaphors are a little mixed, but its brevity is undeniable. Now for the little tale. There was once a wilful, headstrong, reckless, loose-living young man whose name was—whose name was——?

EDANA (*a little drowsily*). Peregrine Hinde.

REV. P. Peregrine Hinde. And he loved with all his heart a beautiful heartless woman, whose name was—whose name was——?

EDANA. Venetia Lee, and she jilted him.

REV. P. She did. And he went about in black despair for months. He thought his heart was broken all to pieces. But it wasn't. He conquered his trouble, and he met another girl who made him a dear, true helpmeet all the years of his manhood. And now when he remembers that old trouble, it's only to think of the use and the beauty of sorrow.

EDANA. What use? What beauty?

REV. P. The use of beautifying our faces. Happiness rounds a face into earthly beauty, but sorrow bravely borne carves it into heavenly loveliness. That's one use. And there's no use in this world so useful as beauty. And another use is to beautify our characters and fortify our spirits. Dear me, dear me, dear me! I'm preaching another sermon. And another use that old troubles have is the use of making a tale to tell to our children over the fire on a winter evening. There! Now for the little song!

(By this time her eyes are closed. He croons out an old country song—stops in the middle of it and looks at her—sees she is fast asleep. A knock at the outer door. Rev. Peregrine Hinde goes to open it, opens it.)

STEPHEN GURDON *enters.*

REV. P.   Stephen!

STEPHEN.   Is the Doctor here?

REV. P.   No, I'm waiting for him.   What's the matter?

STEPHEN.   Jessie's come home.

REV. P.   Jessie!

STEPHEN.   She wants to see a doctor, so I thought I'd come here as Dr. Carey is nearest.   And she said she should like to see you too, pa'son.

REV. P.   Very well, Stephen.   I'll come to her. Is she ill?

STEPHEN.   She ain't in any immediate danger, but she doesn't look as if she'd got many months to live.

REV. P.   Poor child!   Is she changed?

STEPHEN.   She's what you might expect her to be. What would any girl be after five years of that life? What would——

(Glancing very significantly at EDANA, who is sleeping in the armchair.)

REV. P. *(hastily.)*   Hush!   Hush!   She hasn't

slept for three nights! (*Draws the curtains down.*) I
can leave her for a few minutes. Now, Stephen, I'll
go with you!

> (*Exeunt* STEPHEN *and* REV. PEREGRINE
> HINDE *at outer door. A long pause.*)

EDANA (*asleep, moans*). Walter! Walter! Come
away from them! Come! I'll take care of you! Ah!
(*A little shriek.*) Don't hurt him! You don't know
how brave and good he is! Make haste, dear! Make
haste! (*Laughs.*) That's right! Come along!
Dearest! Dearest! Dearest! (*Very caressing, with
movement of stroking his hair with her hand.*) Where
have you been all this while? Why did you leave
me so long? And not a word! Oh, it's cruel!
Don't leave me again! You won't? You won't?

> (*A long moan, then silence. After a long
> pause,* DR. CAREY *enters at inner door,
> goes up to the table in the bay window,
> throws off his hat and overcoat, and puts
> them carelessly on the chair* R. *of table
> in window, takes up a glass slide, puts
> it under microscope, is busy bending over
> it for some seconds.* AMPHIEL'S *face
> appears to the right of the window at
> back, he looks in and creeps stealthily all
> round the window. As soon as he has
> disappeared to the left,* DR. CAREY *shows
> sudden attention as if he were arrested by
> a sound outside. He hastily leaves table*

*and goes to the little window L., looks off.
A gleam of interest, almost triumph,
crosses his face. The handle of the outer
door is fumbled at and half turned. DR.
CAREY watches it. The handle is again
turned, and the door opens (on to the
stage), AMPHIEL'S face being seen by the
audience before it is seen by DR. CAREY.
AMPHIEL looks very haggard and dis-
sipated. His first expression seen by the
audience is watchful, sly, and anxious,
but as he enters, and is seen by DR.
CAREY, he assumes a frank, cordial
manner, goes up to DR. CAREY with
outstretched hand.)*

AMPHIEL (*very cordially*). Ah, Doctor, you got
my telegram——

DR. C. (*refusing his hand*). Yes.

AMPHIEL. I thought I'd let you know I was
coming. I've been working in the good cause. I
knew you wouldn't let me go, so I slipped away.
Won't you shake hands with me and welcome me
back?

DR. C. (*rather sternly*). Where have you been?

AMPHIEL (*with the utmost frankness*). In the West
of England looking after the refuges I started last
year. We've done such good work in Bristol.
(EDANA *stirs a little and moves her hand.*) Why do
you look at me like that?

Dr. C. (*more sternly*). Where have you been?

Amphiel. What makes you so angry with me? Surely you don't suspect—you don't suspect that I've broken my word?

Dr. C. (*very sternly*). Where have you been?

Amphiel. Don't I tell you? I've been engaged in my work.

Dr. C. All the time?

Amphiel. Yes, every day, every hour, almost every minute since I left you. I've done nothing else.

Dr. C. You liar!

> (Edana *opens her eyes and looks round, scarcely awake, listens as if in continuance of her dream, gradually growing more and more interested.*)

Amphiel. You don't believe me? I can give you an account of how I have spent every moment of my absence.

Dr. C. Shall I give you an account instead? Shall I tell you where and how you have spent the last few days? You've been at the Harp in Temple Mead, Bristol, one of the lowest and filthiest dens in the place. Shall I tell you in what condition and in whose company you've been? You've been lying there in a drunken debauch since last Thursday, in the company of sots and harlots, fouling, maddening, destroying yourself.

Amphiel. It's true! It's true! I'm a beast!

I'm a beast! I'm not fit to live—I'll go and end it
this moment. (*Rushing off towards outer door.*)

DR. C. Stop, you fool! There's somebody else
to think of. Do you know what this means to her?
Do you know that she has been night and day on a
rack of suspense? She was here just now begging—
begging me to give her some news of you.

AMPHIEL. You didn't tell her?

DR. C. No. I left that for you to do. Go and
report yourself to her.

AMPHIEL. What do you mean?

DR. C. She must know sooner or later. Do you
think I will let you wreck her life as well as your own?
Do you think I will stand by and let her marry you ;
bear you children that will perhaps inherit your taint
in every bone and nerve, let her watch you sinking
inch by inch into imbecility and corruption, while she
gradually loses all her beauty and trust and love—
Oh, my God! what a gift for a man!—and becomes
a hopeless, wretched drudge to you and your vice
—do you think I'll stand by and see that? Eh,
do you think I will? No! put an end to it. Do
you hear? Put an end to it! She's over at the
Vicarage waiting for news of you. Go and tell her
what you are.

> (EDANA, *who has been listening, amazed and
> horrified, comes to curtains still dazed
> and overwhelmed.*)

AMPHIEL. Very well. You can make me tell her ;

but, mark me, if you do I'll end it. The moment
she knows me for what I am I'll kill myself.

>   (EDANA, *who is about to draw aside the
>   curtains and declare herself, draws back,
>   stands still, horror-stricken, till end of
>   scene.*)

AMPHIEL (*suddenly turns to* DR. CAREY, *with an
outburst of agonised entreaty*). Give me one more
chance! Don't let her know! Give me one more
chance! I'll keep my word this time!

DR. C. Your word!

AMPHIEL. I will! I will! Don't despise me!
I'm not so bad as you think me. Oh, do hear me!
Don't let her know!

DR. C. But to continue to deceive her—the
hypocrisy——

AMPHIEL. I'm not a hypocrite! I've given all
my time and money to save others from this curse!
I'm not a hypocrite; don't think that of me! Oh,
you don't know what awful struggles I've had—how
I've tried and tried and tried to conquer myself.
And I will! I won't give way again! Give me one
more chance! You're my only friend! don't turn
away from me! Give me one more chance, only one,
only one. One more chance, for mercy's sake—one
more chance!

DR. C. And if I did, how could I trust you now?

AMPHIEL. I'll give you my oath. Listen. I
mean it. There's no going back from this. Remember

what I say and bring it up against me. If ever from this time forth one cursed drop shall pass my lips, may I lose her, may I lose my soul and everything that I hold dear in this world and the next. There! I've said it. You believe me? You'll give me one last chance for her sake? One last chance!

DR. C. For her sake, because I put her happiness beyond everything in this world, I will give you one last chance. I'll forget these last few weeks—do you forget them too—and I'll help you again to the very utmost of my power.

AMPHIEL (*bursts into tears*). God bless you! I'll —I'll—I'll——(*breaking down, sobbing and exhausted*). God bless you! You are good to me! and I'll deserve it. I will—I'll—I'll——

DR. C. Come! come! You're too excited. You had better go to rest. Let me get you something after your journey.

AMPHIEL. No. I can't eat. I—I—I——(*clinging to* DR. CAREY *piteously and crying feebly*). Oh, I feel so weak and wretched. I'll get to rest—I'll——

DR. C. Ah, my poor lad, this is a hard taskmaster you've got. You've escaped him this time. Don't fall into his hands again, for he'll have no mercy on you.

AMPHIEL. I won't! I won't! (*Crying.*) Oh, you are good to me. You won't leave me.

DR. C. (*very tenderly*). No, no, I won't leave you. Trust to me. Don't despair. We'll make a fresh start to-morrow. (*Soothing him and helping him to inner door.*) Come, come! Cheer up! There, there! A fresh start! A new life to-morrow.

> (*Helping him off at inner door. Closes it. Comes down stage slowly, reflectively, with anxious face.*
>
> EDANA, *who has stood horror-stricken and quite still behind the curtains, draws them slowly aside. His eye catches the movement of the curtains, and he watches them, sees her standing there.*)

DR. C.   You heard?   (*She signs " Yes."*)

CURTAIN.

(*Nine months pass between Acts III. and IV.*)

ACT IV

Scene—The Vicarage Drawing-Room at Fontleas, a pleasant cosy Room with pretty
chintz Furniture.

*A large window at back looking over a garden in late
summer. A door* R. *A door* L. *Discover* Rev.
Peregrine *up at window, which is open.*

Rev. P. (*calling off towards* L.). Go round, Mrs.
Bowden. Go round and come in !
    (*Crosses to left and opens the door.*)

  Enter Mrs. Bowden *in her Sunday best.*

Mrs. B. (*curtseying*). Good afternoon, pa'son. I
felt I must come and ask after Miss Edana—and
whether she has heard the good news ?
 Rev. P. Good news ?
 Mrs. B. We've just had a telegram from Dr.
Carey. He's coming back to-day. Haven't you
heard ?

Rev. P.   Oh yes.   We've had a telegram too.

Mrs. B.   And of course Mr. Amphiel is coming along with him?

Rev. P. (*rather troubled*).   Oh yes—Mr. Amphiel is coming with him.

Mrs. B.   I was so pleased, because I thought, "There! It's quite a providence Mr. Amphiel coming back just as Miss Edana has got well again. How is she?"

Rev. P.   Much better.   Quite well!   Quite her old self except for a little weakness.

EDANA *enters door* R.; *her features are sharper, and she shows signs of illness and suffering.*

Rev. P.   Here she is!

Mrs. B. (*going cordially to* EDANA).   My dear, I be so glad to see your pretty face again! I must give you a kiss for the sake of old times! (*Kissing her.*) Ah, there's somebody else coming to kiss you this blessed day.

(*A shade of trouble and horror crosses* EDANA'S *face and she turns away.*)

Mrs. B.   And how are you, my dear?

EDANA.   I'm better, thank you.

(*Sits down apart, with a quiet and reserved manner.   Wedding bells ring out.*)

Rev. P.   Dear me!   I was forgetting—I've got to marry James Hebbings and Louisa Pack.—I suppose you're coming to the wedding, Mrs. Bowden?

MRS. B. Yes, to be sure—and aren't you coming, my dear—to see James and Louisa married?

EDANA. No—I'd rather stay at home.

MRS. B. Ah, to be sure! I don't wonder. You're expecting Mr. Amphiel every minute. Let me see—how long is it since he and Dr. Carey went away—it was last December, wasn't it?—How time does slip away!

REV. P. (*trying to get her away from* EDANA). Yes, it does! We ought to be at the church.—Come along, Mrs. Bowden.

MRS. B. (*to* EDANA). Well, good-bye, my dear. I˙ hear poor Jessie Gurdon is very near the end, pa'son.

REV. P. Yes, poor girl! I was with her last night, and I scarcely thought she'd last till this morning.

MRS. B. Oh dear, oh dear! what a world of sin and misery it is, to be sure! It's a good job as there's a better one by and by.

REV. P. It's a bad job, Mrs. Bowden, that folks don't make a good job of this one, here and now.

Enter, L., LIZZIE, *the Vicarage servant*.

LIZZIE. James Hebbings and Louisa Pack would like to see you for a minute before the wedding, sir.

REV. P. Show them in.

H

LIZZIE *beckons off and* JAMES *and* LOUISA *enter,* L., *in their wedding clothes. They are arm-in-arm, and* JAMES *is very much embarrassed.*

JAMES. We've come, pa'son——
> (*Breaks down and has a little fit of foolish giggling.*)

LOUISA (*nudging* JAMES). Do behave yourself, James. (*To* REV. PEREGRINE.) We thought as Miss Edana wasn't coming to the church, we shouldn't like her to miss seeing us in our wedding clothes.
> (*Spreading herself and* JAMES *for* EDANA'S *inspection.*)

EDANA. Thank you, Louisa—thank you, James.
> (*With effort to take an interest.*)

MRS. B. Very sweet, oh, very sweet. Quite taking!   (*Admiring them.*)

JAMES. And also we thought we might akse you, pa'son, whether everything is in good order for the wedding—that is, so fur as your part of these proceedings is concerned. (*Adds thoughtfully*) Thereby.

REV. P. My part of the proceedings shall be duly and punctually performed, James.

JAMES. And ours also.
> (*Suddenly makes a grab at his waistcoat pocket, shows alarm, feels in his pockets, disengages himself from* LOUISA, *fumbles.*)

LOUISA What's the matter?

JAMES. I've lost the ring.

LOUISA. No—no——

JAMES. Yes—no, here it is. That's all right!
I'll make sure of it this time.

> (*Placing it carefully in pocket, keeps one hand
> carefully on the pocket all the remainder
> of the scene.*)

LOUISA. Do behave yourself, James. (JAMES
gives her his arm very ceremoniously.) And we wish
you our best respects, miss. And we thank you for
your beautiful present. And we're so sorry you aren't
coming to the wedding——

MRS. B. Why don't you perk up a bit, my dear,
and come?

EDANA (*quickly*). No, no, indeed I can't. But I
hope you will be very happy.

JAMES (*with a giggle, glancing at* LOUISA). No fear!
And also no fear for you and Mr. Amphiel, miss——

LOUISA. And we hope you'll very soon be married
yourself, miss.

> (EDANA *turns away to window and hides her
> head.*)

JAMES. What's the matter?

MRS. B. Don't you see, you silly chap? It's her
joy that her sweetheart's coming back. He's been
nearly all over the world, and she hasn't seen him for
nine months.

REV. P. (*who has shown sympathy with* EDANA).
Come, I think it's nearly time that we were all over at
the church. Now, James. Now, Louisa.

JAMES (*to* LOUISA).   Have we said anything wrong?
(*Exeunt* JAMES *and* LOUISA *arm-in-arm,*
door L.)

REV. P.   Now, Mrs. Bowden——
(EDANA *is sobbing a little in window.*)

MRS. B.   Good-bye, my dear!   It's joy at the
thought of seeing him !
(*Making a movement to go to* EDANA.)

REV. P. (*intercepting her*).   If it is joy, let it be
sacred.   Leave her to me !

MRS. B. (*snivelling a little*).   I know what it is.
God bless you, my dear.
(*Exit* MRS. BOWDEN *door* L., *leaving the door*
open.)

REV. P. (*to* EDANA).   My dear ! this has been too
much for you.
(LIZZIE *shows in* STEPHEN *by the open door.*
Exit LIZZIE.

REV. P.   Stephen—it's all over ?

STEPHEN.   Yes.   I want a word with you, pa'son.
(EDANA *is going.*)   And with you too, miss.

EDANA.   Poor Jessie is gone ?

STEPHEN.   Yes.   She asked me to thank you, and
you too, pa'son, for all your kindness.   (*A little pause.*)
And I think I ought to tell you——

REV. P.   What ?

STEPHEN.   Last night, in the middle of the night,
she was quite clear and bright, and she looked for a
minute or two like her old self.   She told me the

name of the man who ruined her and took her away from home.

REV. P.   Yes?   Who was it, Stephen?

STEPHEN.   It's the man that's coming back to Fontleas to-day.

REV. P.   Are you sure, Stephen, it was he?

STEPHEN.   She was dying, and she didn't tell me a lie.   You know the man I mean, miss?

EDANA.   Yes.

STEPHEN.   Then I needn't say any more.   That's the man that ruined Jessie and led her into that life of shame.   If you marry him now you marry him with your eyes open.   (EDANA *turns away.*)   I've done right to warn her, pa'son?

REV. P.   Yes, Stephen, you've done right.

STEPHEN.   He's expected to-day, ain't he?

REV. P.   Yes, every minute.

STEPHEN.   I shall have a word to say to him.

REV. P.   No, Stephen, no.   You'll forgive him. Go now; I'll come over to you by and by.

STEPHEN.   I shall have a word to say to him.

(*Exit* STEPHEN, L.)

REV. P.   My poor girl!

EDANA.   Father, I cannot marry him!   I cannot! I cannot!   We were wrong not to tell him before he left England.

REV. P.   We did it for the best.   Dr. Carey said that if he knew you had found him out it would most likely prey upon his mind and drive him to drink and death. And when Dr. Carey offered to give him one more chance and take him away——

EDANA. I think Dr. Carey is the truest and best man that ever lived. I can never thank him enough. But I was wrong to let him go, I ought to have told Walter and broken it off at the time——

REV. P. Suppose you had, and had sent him to despair——

EDANA. He will have to know now. I wonder he hasn't guessed it from my letters. I wonder he didn't guess it when I wished him "Good-bye," for I shuddered and felt—oh, I cannot tell you how I felt—almost as if I hated him. And all these months he has been away, I have felt my dislike for him growing day by day. And he is coming back, as he thinks, to marry me—you remember what he said in his last letter. And Dr. Carey writes that he has really kept his word this time. Oh, tell me what can I do? what can I do? I don't want to be cruel to him—I don't want to drive him to *that*; but whatever happens, I cannot marry him, I cannot! I cannot! I cannot!

Re-enter LIZZIE, R.

LIZZIE. They've sent over from the church, sir. The folks are all there, and they're waiting for you to go on with the wedding.

REV. P. Very well, Lizzie, I'll come at once. (*Exit* LIZZIE, L.) I must go. Don't give way, dear. I'll come back as soon as the wedding is over.

EDANA. And you'll think of some way of breaking it to him without——

REV. P. Without breaking your heart and without breaking his? Yes, I must think of some way. I must think of some way.

> (*Exit* L., *puzzling and anxious.* EDANA, *left alone, goes to table, sits, and buries her face in hands.* DR. CAREY *appears at the window* R., *and watches her with great interest for some moments without her seeing him ; at length, in turning, she catches sight of him ; stops.*)

EDANA. Dr. Carey——   (*A little alarmed.*)

DR. C. (*through the window. He is bronzed as if with a long sea voyage*). May I come in?

EDANA. Is any one with you?

DR. C. No, I am alone.

EDANA. Will you go round?

> (*He disappears at back. Enters* L., *looks at her with great interest, anxiety, longing, and affection.*)

DR. C. Are you better?

EDANA. Yes.

DR. C. No one in the house?

EDANA. No, they are gone to the wedding. Are you alone?

DR. C. Yes—quite—for the time. (*Taking her hands.*) Let me look at you. You've been very ill?

EDANA. Yes. It was that dreadful night. I didn't

feel it at the time, but after you and he had gone, I felt—I——(*Shudders, then suddenly breaks down and sobs out.*)   Oh, I'm so glad you've come back!

(*Sobbing.*)

DR. C.   Come, come, I must have you brave!

EDANA (*a little recovering*).   Where is he?

DR. C.   I've not brought him to Fontleas.

EDANA.   Is he better —well?   ·

DR. C.   Quite well.

EDANA.   Where is he?

DR. C.   I had to hurry to Europe, because I wanted to get to India at once and deal with this fresh outbreak of the plague.   So I had to leave him.

EDANA.   Leave him?   Where?

DR. C.   He hasn't come by this vessel.   He won't be back for some weeks—perhaps months.

(*Watching her very closely.*)

EDANA.   Oh, I'm so glad!

DR. C. (*with a sudden light of hope in his face*). Glad?   (*Looks at her again with anxious interrogation.*) Glad?   (*She nods.*)   Miss Hinde, what do you mean?

EDANA.   I cannot marry him.   (DR. CAREY'S *face brightens with the utmost excitement of hope.*)   I must write and tell him.   Dr. Carey, if he knows that our engagement is broken off and that I can never see him again, will it harm him?   Will it drive him to despair and—worse?

DR. C.   No.

EDANA.   You're sure?

DR. C. Quite sure. Miss Hinde, three days before we sailed, he left me. I feared what had happened. I saw no more of him till an hour before the ship was due to leave. He came on board a perfect wreck : he had been sleeping in the rain, and was very ill——

EDANA. Go on.

DR. C. He had a few days of awful agony and remorse, and then pneumonia set in. He passed away very peacefully (*wedding hymn in church*), and asked me to beg you to forgive him.

EDANA. I forgive him. And you—what will you do?

DR. C. I go to India, unless—unless——

> (*He holds out his arms to her with a gesture of longing entreaty. She goes to him very simply. He utters a great cry of satisfied love as she falls into his arms.*)

CURTAIN.

Printed by R. & R. CLARK, LIMITED, *Edinburgh.*

MACMILLAN AND CO.'S BOOKS ON THE DRAMA.

ENGLISH HISTORICAL PLAYS BY SHAKE-
SPEARE, MARLOWE, PEELE, HEYWOOD, FLET-
CHER, and FORD. Arranged for acting as well as for
reading. By THOMAS DONOVAN. In 2 vols. Crown 8vo.
15s.

By Mr. GOODMAN.

THE KEELEYS: ON THE STAGE, AND AT HOME.
By WALTER GOODMAN. With Portraits and other Illustra-
tions. Demy 8vo. 14s.

By the late Mrs. KEMBLE.

FANNY KEMBLE'S RECORDS OF LATER LIFE.
By FRANCES ANNE KEMBLE. 3 vols. Crown 8vo. 10s. 6d.

. Mrs. Kemble's " Records of My Girlhood " (3 vols.) is now out of print.

FURTHER RECORDS. A Series of Letters by
FANNY KEMBLE, forming a sequel to "Records of My
Girlhood," " Records of Later Life," etc. 2 vols. Crown
8vo. With two Portraits engraved upon steel by G. J.
STODART. 24s.

By THEMSELVES.

MR. AND MRS. BANCROFT : Their Recollections
On and Off the Stage. Eighth Edition. Crown 8vo.
Paper wrapper, 1s. ; or in cloth, 1s. 6d.

By Dr. DORAN.

IN AND ABOUT DRURY LANE, and Other Papers.
By the late JOHN DORAN, F.S.A. 2 vols. Large crown
8vo. 21s.

By Mr. NEVILLE.

THE STAGE. Its Past and Present History in Rela-
tion to Fine Art. By HENRY NEVILLE. Demy 8vo.
96 pp. 5s.

MACMILLAN AND CO., LTD., LONDON.